Jailhouse Golem

Steve Higgs

BOOKS

For no other reason than because I want to, this book is getting dedicated to my son, the thunder hippo. As I finish this book, he is in bed with a cast on his left foot. He was only out of a cast for nine days after breaking his left elbow trying to impress the cute blonde girl from his class who lives next door. He jumped off a platform to elbow drop a rubber hippo.

To break his foot, he tried to jump onto the couch and missed. That's not a very good story though, so when he returns to school for the start of the new term next Monday, I plan to have coached him with a better one. It will involve ninjas, and possibly a tiger, plus a zipline, some explosives, and maybe even a few dinosaurs for good measure.

He is five.

To you, Hunter, you are my greatest inspiration.

Vinci Books

vinci-books.com

Published by Vinci Books Ltd in 2025

1

Copyright © Steve Higgs 2021

The author has asserted their moral right to be identified as the author of this work in accordance with the Copyright, Designs and Patents Act 1988. This work is a work of fiction. Names, characters, places and incidents are the product of the author's imagination or are used fictitiously. Any resemblance to actual persons, living or dead, places and incidents is entirely coincidental.

All rights reserved. No part of this publication may be copied, reproduced, distributed, stored in any retrieval system, or transmitted in any form or by any means, including photocopying, recording, or other electronic or mechanical methods, nor used as a source for any form of machine learning including AI datasets, without the prior written permission of the publisher.

The publisher and the author have made every effort to obtain permissions for any third party material used in this book and to comply with copyright law. Any queries in this respect should be brought to the attention of the publisher and any omissions will be corrected in future editions.

A CIP catalogue record for this book is available from the British Library.

Paperback ISBN: 9781036708689

The EU GPSR authorised representative is Logos Europe, 9 rue Nicolas Poussion, 17000 La Rochelle, France contact@logoseurope.eu

By Steve Higgs

Blue Moon Investigations

Paranormal Nonsense
The Phantom of Barker Mill
Amanda Harper Paranormal Detective
The Klowns of Kent
Dead Pirates of Cawsand
In the Doodoo with Voodoo
The Witches of East Malling
Crop Circles, Cows and Crazy Aliens
Whispers in the Rigging
Paws of the Yeti
Under a Blue Moon
Night Work
Lord Hale's Monster
Herne Bay Howlers
Undead Incorporated
The Ghoul of Christmas Past
The Sandman
Jailhouse Golem
Sparks in the Darkness
Shadow in the Mine
Ghost Writer
Monsters Everywhere

Modern Fairy Tale
No Such Thing as Magic

Albert Smith Culinary Capers

Pork Pie Pandemonium
Bakewell Tart Bludgeoning
Stilton Slaughter
Bedfordshire Clanger Calamity
Death of a Yorkshire Pudding
Cumberland Sausage Shocker
Arbroath Smokie Slaying
Dundee Cake Deception
Lancashire Hotpot Peril
Blackpool Rock Bloodshed
Kent Coast Oyster Obliteration
Eton Mess Massacre
Cornish Pasty Conspiracy
The Gastrothief
Lyme Regis Layover
Majestic Mystery

Maidstone Prison Minimum-Security Wing

THURSDAY, MAY 11TH 1736HRS

Dinnertime came around again as it does every day, and I left my cell to make my way to the mess hall. That I think of it as a mess hall harks back to my Army days. I served for long enough that the names for some things might have stuck in my head and may be there forever.

I sat with other inmates, eating our meals while chatting amiably about this or that or nothing much at all.

In the minimum-security wing, the guard to inmate ratio was even less than I expected, but no one in here was going to misbehave. Most prisoners were serving short sentences and would be home with their families - or whatever they had – soon enough. They just had to keep their heads down and do their time.

The same applied to me, yet my case was a little different from most others. I had enemies inside the walls that housed us all. None were in with me, but the main exercise yard was a large square in the centre of the property where the prison looped around to enclose it on all four sides. The prisoners, separated into different wings, would sometimes pass each other as one came out and the other went in. We were on different sides of a fence, but I got spotted on only my second day inside.

I knew the face but could not put a name to it. He knew me though, shouting my name to the accompaniment of violent threats until two prison officers tackled him. One was a huge man, bigger even than my old army buddy, Big Ben. Not so much in height, though I judged he was a shade taller than Big Ben's six feet and seven inches, but in girth.

Where Big Ben was lean hard muscle, the guard was carrying another hundred pounds which was half fat and half muscle. He looked like a professional rugby player. Or perhaps someone a professional rugby team might take great interest in. However, when the inmate resisted, near foaming at the mouth with his desire to kill me, the guard performed a move I had only ever seen on television.

It caused me to reassess his athletic ability and relabel him as a wrestler. Doubly so when he then put the inmate in a sleeper hold.

'Move along, Michaels.' The instruction came from a prison officer called Gomez. He was friendly, as all the guards in minimum security seemed to be, but they were still prison officers, and I was an inmate.

In many ways, I was here by choice. I knew the probable consequences when I publicly chose to punch a chief inspector in the mouth. I say publicly, but what I mean is I did it live on national television at a press conference. To explain why, I would choose to remind you how a pearl is formed – through constant irritation.

Chief Inspector Quinn was the piece of grit stuck inside my shell, and the punch was my solution. So I was in jail, though to be honest, I was rather enjoying it.

Adjusting to the slow pace of life in prison didn't take

me as long as I expected it to. I had eight weeks to serve; my penalty for putting Chief Inspector Quinn on his backside.

Apparently, he required some dentistry following my single punch, but my hope I might be able to plead I used minimal force fell on deaf ears. Yes, I only punched him once and thus could not have hit him any fewer times. However, I also knocked him out with that first punch and the judge believed it had been premeditated.

I didn't bother to argue; it had been.

They put me in the minimum-security wing of Maidstone Prison. When I get out, I can walk across the road to the bar there and wait for Big Ben, Amanda, and the others to come find me.

I get to read books, and I can use the internet for an hour a day. There was a well-stocked gym I was choosing to visit six days out of every seven and felt certain I was going to drop a few pounds and return home distinctly leaner than I was when I arrived.

Even the food was pretty good, and with the total absence of alcohol from my diet, I was allowing myself the indulgent French toast they served at breakfast each morning. It was the best I had ever eaten.

All in all, getting locked up was a positive experience so far.

I was missing my dogs though. Bull and Dozer were staying with my girlfriend/business partner, Amanda. She was running my paranormal investigation business along with a third detective, my former assistant, Jane Butterworth.

They were more than capable of handling anything that came up in the short time I was stuck inside, and I gave it all very little thought.

In fact, the only thing that made me think of my work

life outside of the jail was a rumour going around of strange occurrences at night.

It started a few weeks ago when a giant man-shaped apparition was seen in the maximum-security wing. I hadn't known about it when they locked me up, but the prison, like so many other old buildings in England, was supposedly haunted, if that is the right word in this case. The ... thing is a golem – a man made from clay and given instruction by its creator. It has been seen many times during the history of the prison and was credited with severely grisly deaths. That's if you are prepared to believe all that nonsense.

I knew basic supernatural lore and legend – I couldn't really avoid picking up some knowledge in my job, but though I was mildly curious about what inmates might have seen, it was largely driven by the desire to debunk it.

When my head hit the pillow that night, I wasn't thinking about a golem though, I was thinking about rum. I wouldn't normally give rum, or alcohol of any kind, the slightest thought on a Thursday night. However, now cut off from the freedom to make choices for myself, I rather fancied a couple of beverages.

My idle fantasies didn't keep me awake for very long.

Rude Awakening

FRIDAY, MAY 12TH 0115HRS

'Michaels.'

The lights in my cell flicked on, bathing me in sudden light that was harsh on my eyes.

On the top bunk, Banksy swore loudly, questioning what might be happening.

I continued blinking, trying to force my eyes to adjust because something unusual was occurring and that was enough to put me on high alert.

I had enemies inside Maidstone Prison as I mentioned earlier. Plenty of them, in fact.

'Michaels, the warden wants you.' Squinting at the door as it swung open and a guard filled it, I could make out the rather tubby form of Officer Gomez.

I rubbed my face and swung my legs around. I'd only been in prison for a week; still settling in, one might say. The time on my watch showed 0115hrs.

Prison Officer Gomez delivered me to the Warden's office, why the man who ran the place was here so late at night only occurring to me to question as we reached his door.

Gomez knocked, waited to be invited in, and announced me.

I hadn't met the warden and never expected to. I was a minor offender in for a short period of time – there was nothing special about me.

So why did the warden want to see me in the middle of the night?

'You can go,' the warden dismissed his member of staff. Gomez closed the door on his way out.

It left just me and the warden in the room. He was looking at me, I was looking at him. He had trim grey hair and a close-cropped, yet full beard. His eyes were a silvery blue and gave the impression he was analysing me every bit as much as I was him. He wore a good suit, cut from a soft grey cloth, and his figure was trim. I guessed his age at mid-sixties and wondered how long he had to go until retirement.

Behind him on the desk, smoke twirled upward from a large cigar. I hated the smell of them and could feel the smoke tickling the back of my throat already. If I were anywhere else, I would complain or leave.

A second passed and I wondered if this was one of those daft power games where he was going to wait until I got bored or nervous and spoke only to then tell me he hadn't given me permission to speak. I just wanted to do my time, but though I had no desire to start acting like *Cool Hand Luke*, I wasn't going to be cowed into acting in a subservient manner.

It turned out I had him all wrong because in the next heartbeat, he crossed the room with his right hand out and reaching for mine.

Jailhouse Golem

'Tempest Michaels,' he greeted me. 'I must say this is a real pleasure.'

'Is it?' I questioned, unsure as to what he might be referring. 'I'm in jail and it's the middle of the night.'

My response made him laugh, a big belly chuckle rumbling through him as he let my hand go again.

'I dare say the experience is rather different for you than for me. I have been a close follower of your work for a year now. Ever since that incident with Richard Claythorn. I read about it in the paper and was gripped. I always felt I missed my calling, you know. I should have pursued a career as a detective and put people behind bars, not made sure they reformed themselves once they were.'

'Warden I am curious to hear why I was summoned.' I hoped it wasn't just so he could meet me because I was getting a weird fanboy vibe. If he asked to take a selfie with me, I wasn't sure how I might react.

Scratch that. I knew exactly how I was going to react. I wanted a week off for each picture.

Unfortunately, that wasn't it.

He turned serious suddenly, everything from the timbre of his voice to the set of his face changed.

'I'm afraid I have need of your skills, Mr Michaels.' I hitched an eyebrow. 'Are you aware of the legend of the prison golem?'

I pulled the eyebrow back down. 'I am, but only in the vaguest manner,' I admitted.

The warden began to tell me a tale and while doing so, he backed away to a cabinet in the corner, from whence he then produced a crystal decanter and two glasses. Without asking, he poured two measures and lifted one for me to take.

I couldn't tell what it might be and was not in the habit

of drinking neat spirits. However, I was also going to be completely teetotal for the duration of my stay so figured I might as well grab the chance to have a drop.

It would have been rude not to. That's what I told myself anyway.

A sniff told me it was brandy – not a spirit I would ever choose - but my attention was on the warden and his story. It went back to the early nineteenth century, making the legend over two hundred years old. A giant form attacked and killed three inmates on July eighth, 1809, tearing their limbs off inside their cells which were still locked when the guards arrived.

Other inmates described the creature having caught a glimpse of it as it passed by the small, barred window of their cell doors. The guards found unexplainable clay footprints leading into and back out of the prison. They terminated at one of the prison's external walls.

There were further incidents over the years, including four more deaths that were attributed to the golem. Each time, the deaths took place in C Wing, the maximum-security area, and on every occasion the footprints were discovered, and a hulking human form was reported.

'The last incident was in 1951,' the warden revealed.

I had a nasty feeling he was about to add something else to that statement.

'That should be the last incident used to be in 1951,' he continued, 'because we had a new one tonight.'

I said a few rude words inside my head.

Keeping the sigh I felt inside, I sought clarification. 'You want me to look into it, Warden, don't you?'

'Look into it?' The warden's eyes sparkled with excitement. 'No, man, I want you to catch it.'

Me and My Big Mouth

FRIDAY, MAY 12TH 0129HRS

My opinion on the matter was of no interest to the warden who had a dead prison officer he was currently keeping quiet from everyone but those few who already knew.

I did, however, feel the need to voice my reservations.

'I must say the legend,' I chose my words carefully because I was sure it was all utter nonsense, 'sounds intriguing, but I am not in C Wing.'

The warden skewed his lips to one side.

'Hmm, yes, that does present a barrier, doesn't it?' He tracked back to his desk where he pressed a button to activate a personal address system. 'Superintendent Yardley to the warden's office, please.'

The door behind me opened mere seconds later, a tall, broad-shouldered man in a starched uniform striding through it with purpose.

'You summoned me, sir?' asked the man, clearly the prison superintendent. He was another man I was yet to meet but had heard the rumours and free advice never to cross the head guard. His tone, the way he addressed the warden, suggested he was not content to be summoned like a dog.

The warden looked beyond me to the man now crossing his office. 'I need you to transfer prisoner Michaels to C Wing, effective immediately.'

My eyebrows went for the sky. 'Whoa there, warden. I'm in minimum security. C Wing is maximum security.'

'It will only be for a short period,' the warden assured me dismissively.

I choked out a laugh though there was nothing amusing about his plan. 'I have ... opponents in C Wing,' I pointed out tentatively. 'Quite a few of them.'

The number, I knew for a fact, was forty-three. For a year, I had been solving cases and seeing to it that I did so in such a way that the people responsible for the crimes I was called to investigate went to jail. There were fourteen former Klowns in C Wing for a start. All former criminals with time under their belt when I caught them, they had chosen to follow a man who brought a plague of terror to the county.

Then there were another dozen followers of the Sandman and the Sandman himself. They had only been in here for a few weeks which meant my face would be fresh in their minds. Add to that list some gangsters from Lithuania who I found beneath Chatham Dockyard - they were using the tunnels as a smuggling route, and you can see how the concept of moving to C Wing was making my pulse race.

I explained this to the warden. He was good enough to listen, but my concerns did nothing to sway his course.

To Superintendent Yardley, he said, 'Make sure he has a suitable cellmate – someone who will be able to keep the others off his back.'

'Claude is without a cellmate, sir.'

The warden nodded with a smile. 'Perfect. Claude will do nicely.'

Claude, huh? Why was an alarm bell ringing in my head? 'Is there a reason why he has no cellmate?' I asked, even though I worried I might not like the answer.

Superintendent Yardley smiled at me. 'His last cellmate met with an unfortunate accident, Michaels.' He gestured with his head – time to go.

The warden was already back behind his desk, his attention on something else. As I got to the door, he called for the superintendent to wait.

'Michaels,' he addressed me. 'I do hope you can solve this thing swiftly. If C Wing is as hostile as you believe, you won't want to be in there for long.'

And there it was, a simple threat, subtly delivered. I was going into maximum security where a platoon of criminals I put away were serving hard time. How many of them would happily kill me if they got the chance?

All I had to do was solve a two-hundred-year-old mystery and catch the person behind a fresh murder.

Super.

Eyewitness Testimony

FRIDAY, MAY 12TH 0204HRS

Gomez was still waiting outside the warden's office, but he wasn't there for me. Yardley told him to get my things and deliver them to C Wing – I wasn't even going back to my cell.

I wasn't going to my new cell either because the superintendent took me to meet some of the inmates who had seen the creature over the last few nights.

On the warden's instruction, four of them had been assembled for me in a single room with one guard per man to keep them company. There was no furniture of any kind in the room, leaving the prisoners to sit on the floor if they didn't want to stand. Three of them were, but on instruction from the guards, they were getting up again as the superintendent led me into the room.

'On your feet,' Yardley barked needlessly since they were already all getting up. 'This prisoner is going to ask you questions about what you saw. You will answer him honestly and immediately. Do not embellish or feel the need to add imagined detail. If you didn't see anything, say so.'

Superintendent Yardley stepped to one side, giving me the floor. The four inmates were all looking my way, but their eyes continued to flit between me and the prison officers, particularly the intimidating superintendent.

'I really need to speak to them one on one and alone.' I knew it was a hopeful request.

'Superintendent or sir,' said Superintendent Yardley. It wasn't a complete sentence and part of me wanted to be pedantic and claim I had no idea what point he was trying to get across. However, I did know, I'd been in the Army with a whole host of other rank-oriented morons.

'Of course,' I replied dutifully. 'My apologies, Superintendent. Can we arrange an interview and perhaps just one guard and one inmate at a time?'

'No.' He didn't give it any thought. 'This is what you have. Interview them or don't. This is a waste of time and resources. Were it not an order from the warden you would already be back in your cell.'

Where I want to be.

I kept my thoughts to myself and sucked on my teeth for a second. If I asked them a question as a group, I would get one big rush of garbled nonsense and each would feed off what the others were saying.

'You first then, please.' I pointed to a man with a tattoo of a spider creeping up the side of his face. 'Let's go to one side,' I checked with the Superintendent. 'I assume that is allowed?'

'Superintendent or sir,' he reminded me with an angry growl.

Staying calm, I said, 'Yes, Superintendent.' I didn't bother to refresh my question. He hadn't answered it, and I no longer cared. I walked across the room to a free space near the door and waited for Spider to catch up with me.

'What's your name?' I asked him.

He grunted, 'Spider Murphy,' and jabbed a thumb at his tattoo as if anyone with eyes could fail to see it. So he was a guy with the last name Murphy who picked up a nickname because of Elvis Presley's song and got a tattoo to drive home the point.

'Tell me what you saw, please.' It was a simple question with a wide funnel to get him started. I was talking in a low tone, keeping my voice just above a whisper so the other inmates would have to strain their ears to hear his responses when he matched me.

'Me and Kev the Knuckle,' he pointed across the room to a man with a weak chin and a receding hairline, 'were asleep in our cell when he heard it.'

'Heard what?' I prompted, trying to get all the detail in order.

'An unearthly groan. Like a crypt door shifting in a graveyard, it was.'

So much for not embellishing. Phantom sounds were easy to produce; a person can download them to a phone and play them over its speaker.

'Go on,' I prompted.

He cleared his throat and licked his lips nervously. It made me think the memory scared him to recall. 'I only caught a glimpse, you understand, as it passed by our cell door.'

'Describe it.'

With nothing to hand to record what he said, I focused on trying to remember his words and closed my eyes to better picture the image.

'It was the biggest thing I'd ever seen,' the man whispered in horror. 'As big as an elephant.'

My eyes snapped open. 'How did it fit in the passageway?'

'Tall,' I mean, Spider corrected himself. 'It was tall. Had to be well over seven feet with hands like steamboat paddles. It must have heard Kev gasp, I reckon, because it snapped its head around to look at us. Cor, I'll never forget those eyes. They were like burning embers glowing orange in its head.'

He continued to add superlatives to his version of what he saw, yet it was little different from what any of them claimed to have seen. The other inmates were Mickey Dolenz – undoubtedly so named because his last name was Dolenz – and Sergeant Harris. It turned out his first name was genuinely Sergeant. Dolenz had seen it across the courtyard. When I asked how, he got nervous and started acting furtive. I suspected he'd been having a sneaky smoke at the window high up on the outer wall of his cell. I didn't make him say it, but he'd been looking outside. His description was much the same as Spider's though he hadn't seen its eyes.

I got to talk to them one at a time and they all had different versions of the same story. They were all convinced what they had seen was indeed a supernatural creature. Dolenz claimed he could see the clay footprints it left behind in the moonlight of the courtyard. I asked him what night that was and memorised his answer for later scrutiny.

To the inmates, they were looking at something that wasn't human - a creature made of clay – a golem.

Mysterious? Yes. Supernatural? Well, you know my opinion on that subject.

I had little to go on but that was often true at the start of a case. I had to ask questions, poke my nose in, and see where that led me.

'I'm done here,' I announced, doubting I had anything left to learn from the inmates' shaky eyewitness reports. 'Can I see where it happened?'

The Shower Room

FRIDAY, MAY 12TH 0256HRS

Is it a daft cliché that he was in the shower room? Jokes about bending down to reach the soap filled my head as I followed the superintendent into the tiled area.

The room was ten yards by eight and had a long row of showers along one wall. There was a row of toilets on the opposite wall but no doors to provide privacy. A series of stainless-steel basins sat back-to-back down the middle. There were no mirrors.

Two of the basins were ruined, crumpled by some huge force to render them unusable. There were no tiles on the walls, which one might expect to find in any other shower room, or they might had been smashed in places too.

There was, however, a crumpled mess in one corner. I'd passed two prison officers on the way in, their faces not only solemn but also grim.

Two more prison officers were standing guard inside though neither seemed to want to get too close to the body and both were facing away from it.

'This is how he was found?' I asked. Looking at bodies

isn't my thing. I'm a detective, not a pathologist or forensic scientist, yet I accept that it is one of the bits that goes with my job sometimes.

This was probably the worst one I had ever seen.

'Yes,' replied Yardley, brimming over with detailed information.

The man had been folded in half so the back of his skull met the heels of his shoes. There was no question he was very dead. Moving around to see his face, I discovered he'd taken a terrible beating too. I already knew from the warden the dead prison officer was a twenty-nine-year-old man called Chris Hyde. He'd worked at Maidstone Prison for four years, moving to the maximum-security wing just eight weeks ago. He was unmarried and had no children which was a blessing in a way. Nevertheless, his death would leave a hole in someone's world.

'Are the police on their way?' I asked.

Yardley didn't answer for a second and when he did, he said, 'You will address me as Superintendent Yardley at all times, Michaels. If I need to remind you again, you will go straight to solitary.'

He didn't bother to ask me if that was clear, and I didn't give him the chance.

'Are the police on their way, Superintendent Yardley?'

Focused on the body and not the senior prison guard, I nevertheless heard the rumble in his chest when he growled. 'They have been informed.'

He didn't like me. Or maybe he didn't like anyone. Or maybe his job simply dictated that he had to be surly and aggressive to survive. I wasn't going to walk a mile in his shoes to find out.

I also wasn't going to touch the body – doing so would contaminate the scene, and I didn't have a phone so I couldn't take any pictures. All I could do was commit as much as possible to memory. What I noted most was the terrible damage and the presence of clay.

Coming into the shower room, Superintendent Yardley insisted I avoid stepping on the clearly visible clay footprints. They were twice the size of my foot and only led outward – there were none going in, which led me to question if there was another door.

There wasn't.

'What time did this happen?' I wanted to know, adding, 'Superintendent Yardley,' after a pause. I hadn't thought to ask that question earlier – the difficulty of not having my trusty notebook.

Looking uncomfortable for the first time, Yardley said, 'I believe it was around midnight. He was not due to patrol at that time and no prison officer travels alone in C Wing. However, his absence from the guards' common room was noticed just after 1230hrs this morning. A search was instigated when he failed to respond to his radio. He was found here shortly after one o'clock.'

I made to move forward and found my path blocked by Yardley's arm.

'Superintendent Yardley I need to inspect the body.' I really didn't want to, truth be told. 'And I really need to have a good look around the crime scene.' I was hoping to find traces of grey paint or whatever they had used to create the dead effect on the man pretending to be a golem.

'You're not giving the orders, Michaels,' he rumbled. 'You'll do as I say.'

With an internal sigh, I turned around to face the superintendent. 'I have no desire to investigate this case, yet it appears to be that I am tasked to do so and trapped here among men who wish me harm until such time as I do,

Superintendent Yardley.' I was going to keep saying his name until he got bored with it or grew up a little. 'If I am to be continually hampered, how am I to achieve that aim?'

I guess he didn't like being questioned because he chose that moment to close the distance between us.

I thought he was going to try to hit me. My muscles tensed as an automatic reaction, and a fleeting question shot through my head as I wondered how long I might spend in solitary for putting the head guard on his butt.

There was no attempt to lash out physically though. He didn't even prod me as he rasped into my face, 'My men can solve this mystery, Michaels. Some fancy paranormal detective who got his name in the papers a few times doesn't impress me.'

'Send me back to minimum-security?' I suggested.

Perhaps sensing he had failed to make me cower and was losing face before his subordinates, he straightened again, taking his face away from mine.

'The warden wants you here. Here is where you will stay. I am ordered to assign you two guards to assist you in your ... *investigation*.' He said the word as if it left a bad taste in his mouth. 'Otherwise, you will be subject to the same restrictions as all other members of C Wing and will have to conduct your investigation as best you can.'

There was to be no help in other words. A few hours ago, I had been happily getting more sleep than I was used to and – in an odd sort of way – enjoying my time inside. It was a new experience, and I was making the most of it.

Now I was stuck in a bad situation that threatened to continue until my sentence was complete.

Accepting my fate and sticking my brain back into gear, I asked, 'How did it escape? There are cameras all over the prison and it is a sealed system,' it had to be, or it would literally be the worst prison ever, 'so how is it that no one knows where a seven foot something giant clay man went?'

The answer was that no one knew, just as no one knew how it had gotten inside. There was video camera footage from all over the prison and there were a team of the guards going over it already.

'Is there anything else you need here?' Yardley asked.

I shook my head. 'No, Superintendent Yardley. I ask that I be permitted to talk to the forensic scientists and the police when they arrive.'

He narrowed his eyes. 'I will see what can be done.' Raising his voice, he called out. 'Markham.'

Chaperone

FRIDAY, MAY 12TH 0322HRS

Prison Officer Markham turned out to be the giant bear of a man I labelled as a wrestler just a few hours ago. Up close he was even more imposing.

Superintendent Yardley handed me over. 'Senior Prison Officer Markham volunteered as your liaison and chaperone, Michaels. He will be accompanied by Prison Officer Soliman.' Yardley indicated a regular sized man standing in Markham's shadow.

I nodded silently at them both, wondering what kind of help Markham might actually be. Yardley claimed the man volunteered, but given the superintendent's attitude toward me, I had to question if he picked the biggest man on his crew and ordered him to mess me around.

It turned out I was wrong. Markham was one of the only guards with any trace of humour about him. I got a wink when we first locked eyes and once away from the rest of the officers, he proved to be almost chatty.

'Do you think you can catch it?' he asked, leading me to my new cell.

'Him,' I replied.

'Hmm?'

I repeated myself. 'Him. It's not an it. This golem thing will prove to be nothing more than a superstitious old legend.'

'But what about the glowing eyes?' It seemed Officer Markham was ready to believe.

'Did you see them?' I asked.

'Well, no …'

I continued to press my point, 'Did anyone?'

He changed tack. 'What about the clay footprints? They go right across the yard outside and up to the wall. I reckon it's gone back to the river.'

From behind us, Prison Officer Soliman spoke up for the first time, 'Shut up, Markham. Why would it be going to the river?'

Markham twisted his torso to look at his colleague as he walked. 'The wall points that way. I looked it up once. The golem always goes to that wall.'

'Looked it up?' the other officer questioned.

'Yeah. There's loads of information on the internet. Did you know Kent is the most haunted county in England? There are more haunted castles here than anywhere else on the planet.' Markham was a fan of the subject, clearly. Perhaps that was why he volunteered.

I chose to interrupt. 'I need to get a sample from those footprints.'

Officer Markham sucked some air between his teeth. 'Well, technically …'

'Forget it,' snapped his partner. 'Maximum-security prisoners are not allowed in the yard after dark. Yardley would string us up.'

'How am I supposed to investigate?' I stopped walking

to express my frustration and got a warning look from Soliman for my trouble.

As it turned out, we were already at my cell.

'Here you go,' said Markham, using his radio to ask for the cell door to be opened.

Hearing a questioning rumble of a confused bass voice coming from inside the cell, I remembered my new cellmate, Claude.

'Pleasant dreams,' smirked Soliman.

The cell door popped open just as the man on the bottom bunk was rolling off his bed.

He stood up, unfolding to his full height. Actually, that should be almost to his full height because he had to tilt his head to one side so it wouldn't scrape the ceiling.

I said a bad word.

'In you go,' insisted Officer Soliman. 'Claude won't bite.'

'Oh, yeah?' I questioned as I stepped over the threshold. 'What will he do?'

Claude

FRIDAY, MAY 12TH 0349HRS

Claude looked down at me. I'm six feet tall give or take a fraction of an inch and my eyes didn't reach Claude's nipples. My friend, Big Ben, stands six feet seven inches tall and will forever hence forth be known as Wee Man.

I guessed Claude's height as somewhere close to seven and a half feet. He was broad too, but he wasn't carrying much excess weight. What there was of him appeared to all be muscle.

My lips twitched in a wry smile when the cell door closed behind me and the light went out. There was moonlight coming through the small window behind Claude's head – enough to see by at least. The smile came from a memory of watching prison movies at some point in the past.

Common theory holds that in order to do well, I needed to find the biggest badass in the prison and make him my bitch. Upon doing that, I would be able to go where I wanted and pass untouched because my status as top dog would demand respect.

I didn't see a way to make that happen. For instance, assuming I could get my foot to go high enough to kick Claude in the nuts, I expected, given proportions, for them to be roughly the size of bowling balls. The effect then might be much the same as swatting a T-Rex with a rolled-up newspaper and telling it to behave.

I did not like my chances.

Neither one of us had moved or spoken in over a minute.

'You okay with the top bunk?' he asked me.

The suddenness of his words combined with the softness with which they had been posed caught me by surprise. It was like finding a crocodile who could sing soprano.

'Sure,' I blurted.

The giant man slid back onto the bottom bunk, folding his giant frame in a complicated fashion so he could fit.

'Do introductions in the morning,' he rumbled. 'Good night.'

Feeling like I'd fallen through the looking glass, I echoed his words. 'Yeah, good night.'

I was supposed to be investigating the golem, yet locked in a cell, I could do nothing but think about what I had seen so far and how my new cellmate needed only a coating of clay and a pair of glowing orange eyes to transform into the very thing Spider Murphy and the other inmates described.

There being nothing else to do, I gave the pillow a couple of whacks, settled my head onto it, and went to sleep.

Half an hour later I was woken again when the lights came on. Tonight was not a night for getting sleep.

Markham was back. 'The police have agreed to see you,' he announced through the door.

'Let's go, Michaels,' called Soliman from outside in the corridor.

Blowing out a frustrated breath, I dropped lightly down to the floor and straightened my prison jumpsuit.

Claude was awake but had nothing to say and made no attempt to get up as they opened the door and let me out.

It was time to start poking my nose in.

The Police

FRIDAY, MAY 12TH 0423HRS

On the way to meet the police, I got to ask a bunch of questions. The answer was no to every last one of them.

I wasn't allowed a pen, or a notepad – why would I want a note pad if I couldn't have a pen? A pen makes a good shank. I couldn't have an electronic tablet to record information on – the hard plastic case would make a good shank. The same was true for a piece of chalk apparently and I began to wonder if they might consider a banana a potentially dangerous weapon.

To aid me in my investigation, where recording data for analysis was arguably paramount, I was going to be given nothing at all. My eyes and ears and what was in my head were to be my only tools.

Perfect.

The guards led me back to the shower room. Voices were echoing out from inside this time and the flash of a camera recording the scene shot bright light back into the dim corridor as we approached.

Inside, I was pleased to see faces I recognised. The

crime scene team consisted of two guys in their late forties. I knew them as Steven and Simon and had come to meet them through my girlfriend/business partner Amanda because she was a former cop.

I knew one of the detectives too, though only loosely.

I got a nod from him when he looked around and spotted me.

'I heard you were in here,' said Detective Sergeant Mike Atwell. 'I didn't expect to see you though. How long did you get?'

'Eight weeks.'

He nodded, acknowledging my reply without comment.

'I figured you would be in minimum-security.'

I couldn't help the snort of sad laughter I gave him. 'I was. Now I am not. The warden wants me to catch his golem.'

'This is Detective Constable Becky Martinez,' he nodded with his head at a woman in her twenties. She was standing over by the crumpled form of the dead prison officer in the corner and asking something about what she was seeing.

Simon, on his hands and knees to examine the body said, 'Defensive wounds for sure. He tried to fight whoever it was.'

Speaking quietly so as not to disturb their work, I asked Mike, 'Any hair and fibre that's not his? Anything that might be of help?'

He gave a small shake of his head. 'Nothing yet. Listen, Tempest, I don't mind that you have been tasked to look into this case, but I asked the prison officers to fetch you as a courtesy to the warden only. I have no information to share with you at this time.'

I got what he was saying. We only knew each other in

passing – our paths had crossed a few times, and he was letting me know he was under no obligation to share his investigation findings with me. To do so would just create extra work for him.

I really was on my own.

Trying my luck, I asked, 'Since I am here, can I ask a few questions?'

He gave me a half-shrug - he wasn't going to stop me.

'Hey, guys,' I raised my voice to get their attention. Both Steven and Simon turned to look. 'Have you looked at the footprints yet?'

They looked at each other first before Simon answered.

'Yes. It's local clay. We will need to do some work back at the lab – we have a dirt guy. He'll be able to work out exactly where it came from. Why are you in prison gear?'

Steven answered for me. 'Because he knocked out Quinn, dummy.'

As if the memory came suddenly flooding back, Simon said, 'Oh, yeah. Are you investigating?'

I sighed. 'Yup.'

'Even though you are locked up?'

'Yup.'

That ended the Q & A session. They were only just getting started and I wasn't going to get to look at the evidence anyway. Even if they wanted to share, Quinn would have their jobs if they did.

In the morning, I would start to investigate and piece together what might have occurred. I didn't think for one minute there was a clay man brought to life to kill a prison guard, or that the original legend had anything other than a large, violent man behind it.

That left a plain, vanilla human being, but one capable

of folding a man in half to snap his spine backwards. Heading back to my cell, I already knew exactly where to find one of those.

Old Friends and New Acquaintances

FRIDAY, MAY 12TH 0845HRS

It was so close to dawn by the time I got back to my bed that I didn't bother trying to get any more sleep. Consequently, I was first up, using the stainless-steel basin in our cell to shave and brush my teeth. There was a sheet of steel attached to the wall to act as a mirror. It didn't exactly work, but it was all I was going to get.

I found it ironic that I was missing my old cell and the minimum-security wing.

By the time my cellmate rolled off his bed, I had been up an hour, performed several hundred sit-ups, press-ups, and other exercises and was getting hungry.

'I'm Claude,' he announced, making no attempt to shake my hand. 'Don't touch my stuff.'

'Tempest Michaels,' I replied. 'What happened to the last guy?'

Claude had his back to me as he used the stainless-steel toilet. He was, however, good enough to reply, 'He touched my stuff.'

That was the extent of our conversation and a minute

later a buzzer signalled the start of the day. I sucked in a deep breath when my cell door opened. How far would I get before someone recognised me?

If they picked a fight with me, what would be the outcome with regards to my time inside? Would I be considered equally guilty and get time added on for bad behaviour?

All these questions and many more swirled like a maelstrom inside my head as I followed the crowd to the breakfast line. The smell of bacon and frying grease filled the air. There was no French toast though – I guess the nastier criminals were not deemed worthy. I wanted to fuel myself up, so I took as much as I was allowed and looked about for a place to sit.

That was when it happened.

A pair of eyes popped out of their skull, the owner of the eyes nudging the man next to him feverishly.

It took me a second to dredge his name from the back of my brain: Max Travers. I last saw him across the table in an interview room in Maidstone Police Station. He was one of the Klowns. How many others were about to react?

'Tempest Michaels,' he grinned, stating my name loudly enough for everyone in a five-yard radius to hear. 'This is a nice surprise.'

His breakfast got abandoned as he started toward me and I looked around for somewhere to put mine. Faces were all turned inward, all the inmates looking to see what might happen.

Guards were looking too but none were moving to intercept yet. A glance at the nearest made me frown; he was looking elsewhere as if trying to find someone.

Max kept coming, weaving through the tables and the jostle of inmates moving to find a seat. Others joined him, their faces unfamiliar and unimportant to the matter at hand because they were coming for a fight and it didn't look like anyone was going to stop it from happening.

Adrenalin flooded my body, making my hands tremble involuntarily. It wasn't fear exactly; it was my body's response to the threat. It was powering up my reactions and getting me ready for what was to come.

A man stepped directly in front of me. He was short enough that I could see straight over his head at the change his presence made to Max's face. Full of vigour and righteous vengeance one moment, the next, Max looked like he wanted to be somewhere else. Two more men came to stand either side of me. Both were heavily tattooed and displayed that dangerous bruiser swagger. To me it suggested they were not only used to fighting but liked to do so. They wanted Max to keep coming.

'Go back to your seat now, Maximillian. There's a good chap,' the short man instructed in perfectly clipped English. He sounded like a schoolboy from Oxford.

'He put me in here,' Max argued, unwilling to be put off so quickly.

The man replied calmly, 'I shall not expect to ask you again.'

The men behind Max had already become ghosts, fading into the prison's population as if they had never been there.

Max flicked his eyes up from the short man to my front. They met mine and then flicked back down again. He opened his mouth to say something, thought better of it, and wandered away with only the briefest of glances over his shoulder.

What was I supposed to say at such a juncture? Thank you felt appropriate, but would I then be acknowledging that I fell under the short man's protection? What would be the ramifications of that?

Honestly, prisons are harder to figure out than women. I needed a handbook for both.

The short man turned about. He was the one the guard had been looking for. Was he the governor here? I'd never been able to figure out how an inmate could run things inside a prison and be able to achieve enough influence that running things included the prison officers employed to keep the inmates in check.

He looked at me but before I could speak he nodded his head at the man to my left, and then the one to my right.

'Thank you, gentlemen.'

Dismissed, both men turned and went back to their breakfasts.

'Good morning,' the short man greeted me. 'I'm Henry Featherstone the Third. My associates are Harker and Bowman.'

I squinted at him just a little, but faced with a person being polite, I matched his manners.

'Good morning. I'm ...'

'Tempest Michaels,' he completed my sentence. 'Sent by the warden to investigate the golem. Yes, I know all about you. You have an eight-week sentence which you are now eight days into. It seems that you are to reside in C Wing until you are either released or you catch the golem. I rather think it should be the latter, wouldn't you agree, Mr Michaels?'

Now my eyes reached full squint. Whoever he was, apart from quite obviously the apex prisoner, he was giving me a thinly veiled order.

'I'm not sure that is within my power to achieve,' I countered, choosing my words carefully.

A smirk tilted his lips. 'Do you think me allowing your ... *friends* to become reacquainted with you is in your best interest?' It came with a smile, but it was a threat, nonetheless.

'Why do you want me to catch the golem? Do you know who it is? Can you steer me in the right direction?' Henry's involvement had to be self-motivated, surely? If he knew anything, I wanted to know it too.

Henry Featherstone considered my questions before saying, 'Who can know the mysteries of the supernatural, Mr Michaels? I am led to believe it is your field of expertise and that you do not believe in it. I will say only that it will serve you well to attend most vigorously to solving this case.'

I drew in a slow breath. This was more like it. I might be swimming in the most dangerous waters ever, but I knew a lie when I heard one. The apex prisoner was hiding something. He wanted me to catch the golem just as much as the warden, but he didn't want to tell me why.

I shot him a smile and repeated a line I'd used more than once since I arrived. 'I just want to do my time.'

My statement got a nod of approval. 'Then you may walk freely in C Wing, Tempest. No harm will befall you provided you are diligently pursuing a swift end to the golem mystery. I will be most ... displeased should I hear of another attack.'

I couldn't know if the promise to be able to walk freely in C Wing was his to grant or not. Could he really control all these animals? The threat of his displeasure though, I could imagine how that might go. Harker and Bowman were like two Rottweilers, placid and docile until told to be otherwise.

Just how do I find myself in these situations?

Camera Footage

FRIDAY, MAY 12TH 1442HRS

I spent most of the morning in my cell, tucked out of the way and pondering what my best course of action might be. Whatever I chose, investigate or not, I would be dancing to someone's tune which left me attempting to decide which served me better.

Lunch came and went. An hour of supervised exercise in the yard too. Claude was monosyllabic. It wasn't just that he ignored me – I didn't see him talk to anyone. He spent most of the day in the cell too, reading a book studiously.

Though I was yet to get stuck into my investigation, the golem case seemed simple enough. Someone was taking advantage of an old legend to cover up a murder. The clay footprints would prove to be applied by a device of some kind or maybe the man dressed as the golem really was covered in clay and left it wherever he went. The glowing eyes the inmates saw would be a clever mask with some electronics wired in.

The uncomfortable feeling that Claude matched the physical profile they described continued to worry me.

Strangely, no one else saw the connection and I was choosing to sit on my suspicions for now because if I was right, my presence in his cell was far from coincidental.

Even though I truly didn't want to investigate, I felt I had no choice, but without Markham to act as my chaperone, I couldn't go anywhere except around C Wing. I'd expected to be with him all day, in the prison library, or on the phone to get answers, but until he appeared, I could do nothing but wait.

I wasn't hiding in my cell, and you can't prove I was.

It was after 1400hrs when he finally showed up at my cell. The control room was finally ready to let me see the recorded camera footage.

Being allowed into the control room was a rare honour, Markham told me on the way there. He'd just come back on shift at 1400hrs, and they'd been waiting for him to arrive so he could be the one handling me – Yardley insisted upon it.

It was another example of how the superintendent wanted to hamper me. What did he gain by it?

On the way to the control room, I asked about Henry Featherstone the Third.

Officer Markham flared his eyes. 'You don't want to mess with him,' he warned.

'Okay. Can you tell me why not? Why would he be so invested in me catching the golem?'

Markham frowned - my claim was unexpected.

'It's well known he controls the flow of goods into and out of the prison. If there are drugs coming in, he's behind it. It makes him powerful. And he's backed by 'family' connections on the outside with protection to guarantee his safety on the inside.'

The disbelief at what I was hearing made my face screw

up on itself. 'If it's well-known he's behind it, why isn't he stopped?'

Silent as always until he had something he wanted to say, from behind us Soliman chipped in his thoughts.

'Because there is nothing to connect one to the other. A prison is a tiny microsystem where a different set of rules apply. Just because we know it is him, doesn't mean we can prove it. The drugs, and anything else coming into the prison, are moved by minor players and when we do catch them, which is rare, they would never roll on Henry Featherstone or any of the others.'

I let it go. We were at the control room anyway.

We were expected, but were made to wait until the senior person in the room, a stern woman in her fifties, was ready to let the three of us in.

'This is the one?' she asked, making it clear from her tone that she was unhappy about having to entertain me.

'Good afternoon,' I addressed her directly despite being rudely ignored.

Her head snapped around, her eyes piercing me.

I smiled and thought about giving her a pinky wave.

She growled, 'Put him over there,' gesturing to a chair set before a bank of monitors.

One of her underlings set me up so I could review the footage myself. There wasn't much of it, which is to say there were endless hours of camera feedback, but only a single shot where the golem had been captured.

Cameras are not positioned everywhere as you might imagine, and there are none in the shower room. There is one outside though which caught an image of the creature as it ran from the room.

It was black and white and poor quality – I guess prisons make no profit and thus struggle for budget. The glowing eyes were there for me to see though, appearing as two bright white orbs in the thing's face.

The footage could be paused but they had no facility to print a still. It left me having to memorise the face. Assuming I was looking at a mask, the figure before me matched Claude's dimensions closely enough that it could be him.

Keeping that in mind, I explored the footage a little further.

I learned there were cameras at every intersection, in the main halls where the prisoners would congregate and at the entrance point to the wing. The passage of the golem as it made its way to the shower room and then ran from it should have been caught on camera. However, apart from the one shot right outside the shower room, every camera filled with static as the golem came near it.

At least, that was what people were guessing.

The golem appeared for a half second before the screen scrambled. Thereafter, they were tracking its journey by looking at which camera malfunctioned next. They were only out for a few seconds as if the golem was able to interfere with the electronic signal.

I had an alternate theory which I kept to myself.

Accepting defeat on the camera feed, I asked, 'Is there a schematic I can use to see his route, please?'

Markham and Soliman were over by the door we came in through, taking no part in what I was doing and chatting with another of the guards. My question had been aimed at the man to my left.

The name on his uniform was Holland.

Without answering me, he clicked a button on the console – which I had been expressly forbidden from touching – and a floor plan appeared on a screen to my right.

I said, 'Thank you, sir,' in an absent-minded way, my attention already attuned to work out the golem's route. Jabbing a finger at the screen, I asked, 'That's the shower room right there?'

I got a nod. 'Yes.'

In total, the fuzzy picture occurred four times. By checking the time in the bottom corner of the screen, I could see the sequence of cameras and thus its route. The distance it covered told me it was running. Not a flat-out sprint, but the lumbering, loping run of an over-sized person trying to get somewhere in a hurry.

Supernatural creatures have no reason to hurry, especially ones capable of vanishing into thin air as this one appeared to have done.

Tracing his route with a finger, he entered a hallway with cells on both sides but vanished before he got to the next camera.

I went back to the one shot we had. The picture quality was terrible, but it looked like a man made of clay to me.

Pushing back my chair, I said, 'I need to make a phone call.'

Soliman took no time to consider my request. 'No. No calls. You get one call a week.'

'Then you make it,' I replied, attempting to keep the irritation from my voice. 'There is a killer in the prison, and I'm supposed to work out who it is and how he escaped. He vanishes into thin air between two cameras in a corridor that has no other exits. Will he strike again? Will it be another guard who is killed?'

Soliman was ramping up to retort until Markham cut him off.

'Who do you want to call?'

Somebody on the Inside

FRIDAY, MAY 12TH 1552HRS

Officer Markham made the call using his phone, which was within the rules, he claimed, because I didn't speak to the person at the other end at any point. He arranged for them to come to the prison for visiting time in an hour.

Task complete, I asked to be taken to the passageway where the golem vanished. On the way there, I had another question for them.

'How is it that no one is looking at Claude? How many other seven-and-a-half-foot tall monster inmates do you have?'

Soliman sneered. 'That was everyone's first assumption, Michaels. But it wasn't him. It can't have been.'

I asked the obvious question, 'Why not?'

'He was locked in his cell,' replied Soliman doing nothing to hide the exasperation in his voice. All the inmates were. It was the first thing the on-duty guards checked when they heard the first reports of a giant clay man last week. Your inmate, Claude Monet was safely tucked up in his bed then and again last night when Hyde was killed.'

Fair answer, but it didn't satisfy me. 'You'll forgive me, but how do we know someone didn't open his cell? You opened it to put me in this morning, so why couldn't someone have done that to let him out? They let him out, dress him up, he kills Hyde, and they lock him away again.'

'Only Control can open the doors. Well, Yardley has a master key, but otherwise, the only way out is to ask Control to open the lock. They are all electronic.' It was Soliman who answered yet again, which surprised me because Markham was the chatty one. When I turned to look, the big man had a ponderous look on his face as if he'd just thought of something and now found it completely absorbing.

I didn't have an argument for Soliman; not one I hadn't already voiced. I suspected my cellmate and doubted it was that hard for someone on the prison staff to work out how to circumvent the systems. That the camera feed went dodgy as soon as the golem came near it was already triggering an alarm in my head.

We were entering the corridor where the golem vanished, and I paused to check something on the corner of the wall. It was a smudge of grey matter. If I had my shoulder bag with me, I would have extracted a plastic bag to gather a sample. With nothing to hand, I picked at it with a thumbnail instead.

It crumbled to fine dust as it came free, forcing me to move fast to get my other hand underneath to catch some. Using a little bit of saliva, I rubbed the grey powder into my palm.

'Clay,' I murmured to myself.

'It's the golem all right,' whispered Markham as if the creature might hear him. 'Back to claim another victim.'

'Oh, do shut up, Markham,' sighed his partner and the two fell to bickering.

'What do you think it is then, Mr Smarty-pants?'

'It's not a two-hundred-year-old man made of clay, is it?'

I ignored them, moving into the passageway where the golem vanished as they argued behind me.

The alarm in my head continued to sound because someone on the prison staff was behind Hyde's death. Claude was the weapon they chose for the murder and just as guilty unless it could be proven he was under duress.

I thought about some of the other details I had learned. Yardley had a universal key to open the doors and he didn't want me to solve the case. That wasn't the same as not wanting Hyde's murderer caught, but he was more inclined to have his own men figure it out.

There was no sign they were trying to, though.

The apex prisoner, Henry Featherstone, wanted me to solve the case swiftly though I knew not why. That the golem had been spotted several times before he struck was troubling too. Why appear but do nothing? What did the person behind this gain?

One thing was for certain, I had no idea who I could trust and that included the prison officers.

Bringing my attention back to the here and now, there was nothing special about the passageway that I could find. It was a straight line from one end to the other and roughly fifty yards long. It would have taken the golem maybe ten seconds to get to the camera at the far end but of course he never reached it.

The camera had a time display on it which never

twitched on the playback. However, if I had been looking at doctored footage, then so were the police, and they would have the technology to figure it out soon enough.

I chose to believe what the camera showed which meant the golem stopped before he reached the far end of the corridor.

'Are all these cells empty?' I asked, raising my voice to be heard over the argument still raging between my chaperones.

'Yes,' snapped Soliman. 'The maximum-security wing is operating at seventy percent capacity while new guards are recruited. There just aren't enough people who want to be prison officers.'

The golem ran to a passageway he knew to be devoid of prisoners and vanished by the time the chasing guards caught up to him. Recalling the footage in my head, there had been four prison officers who gave chase. They were more than ten seconds behind which meant that they came into the passageway and ran right through it assuming the golem had too.

If he ducked inside a cell, he would have been able to sneak out again later.

It required someone to operate the cell doors and a way to change his appearance. Not only that, given his size, even dressed differently, he would be hard to hide. No giant form appeared on the footage after the event as the golem (still Claude in my head) snuck away back to their cell, but I knew better than to believe what I was being shown.

At each cell door, I looked inside, though after a few I accepted I wasn't going to be able to see anything through the tiny hatch at eye level.

'Can we get these open?' I enquired, adding, 'The golem had to have hidden in one of them to evade the guards and avoid the camera at the other end. Someone in the prison operated a door to get him in and out again. That person is behind this.'

Markham and Soliman looked at each other. I had made a bold statement, levelling an accusation against the people who were supposed to maintain order inside the prison.

Soliman broke the silence. 'Only Superintendent Yardley can authorise that.'

He didn't say it, but it felt like a big fat, 'No.'

Visiting Time

FRIDAY, MAY 12TH 1600HRS

As if I didn't have enough to think about already, I now had the Superintendent to consider. That he was behind it made sense of his attitude toward me yesterday. He was complying with the warden's instructions regarding my investigation but in the most limited way.

It really made no difference though. I was going to have to point the finger at someone, it might as well be him. I needed evidence yet, but that was going to have to wait because my visitor had arrived.

The visitor area was set up just like one might expect from seeing such things on TV. A glass partition separated inmates from loved ones with opaque panels providing a small amount of privacy as they divided the space into narrow booths.

I sat down and picked up the phone to speak to the man sitting opposite me.

'Hi, Frank.'

'Wotcha, Tempest. How's the food?'

'Plentiful,' I gave him an honest answer. Frank Decaux

owns and runs an occult bookstore in Rochester a few yards from my office. He's the exact opposite to me on the belief system because he thinks everything supernatural, alien, or weird must be true.

He is my walking paranormal encyclopaedia. Markham primed him when he made the call, so Frank knew what he was here for.

'I was able to find lots of references to the golem,' he let me know, excitement at the possibility of a new and dangerous creature making his eyes twinkle. 'It has claimed twelve victims so far if we include the latest one. That's not been released to the press yet, by the way.'

'Were there any investigations into it in the past?' This was one of the questions I'd already primed him to answer, but he knew me well enough to understand the type of detail I required.

'There were,' he squeaked, giddy with the thrill he felt. 'In 1809 when it first struck, the golem took three victims. Each of them was an inmate. The investigation fell to a man called Douglas Keane. He was a special investigator sent from Scotland Yard. Of course, it wasn't called Scotland Yard back then because the police headquarters was in Whitehall. They didn't move to the area of Scotland Yard until 1829.'

I held up a hand. 'Our visitation window is limited, Frank.'

'Yes, sorry, stick to the point. Righto. Keane believed the monster, as it was listed back then, was another inmate but his report shows that no one of that size was incarcerated. Men that were seven feet tall just didn't exist back then. The statements taken from prisoners all claimed the golem left a trail of wet clay footprints.'

'Yes, we have them again here.'

Frank squeaked, his excitement bubbling over. 'Do you have any pictures?'

I rolled my eyes. 'No, Frank. I'm in prison.'

'Oh. Yes, good point. Anyway, the injuries the victims suffered were horrendous. Snapped limbs, a head turned through a hundred and eighty degrees, that sort of thing. Keane's reports were published in two books that I could find. One,' he held it up, 'is Edgar Frobisher's pioneering work *Most Haunted England*. I had a quick read before I came over just to refresh my memory. Keane believed it was a man, not a monster, and that the size had been vastly exaggerated.'

'That's not the case this time,' I let him know. 'I saw camera footage.'

'Gosh,' gasped Frank. 'Well, Keane never did solve the case which leads me nicely to the next piece of juicy information. Golems are as close to indestructible as you can get.' His hands vanished beneath the counter on his side again, reappearing with a different book.

'*Golems: The Most Ancient Monsters*,' I read the cover.

Frank nodded his head vigorously. 'Made of earth or minerals and controlled by whoever creates them, Golems are not alive and therefore cannot be killed. If you chop a part off, a new piece can be added in its place. These things aren't just hard to kill Tempest, they are all but impossible.'

'All but,' I repeated his words. 'How does one kill a golem then.' I had no use for the information but had to admit I was curious to hear his answer.

'Fire,' Frank's eyes danced as if they were backlit by a flame themselves. 'It has to be sustained though. You need to trap the golem and build a fire around it or find a way to draw the golem into a fire and keep it there.'

'Okay, Frank, but let's assume that just like always, this is just a man in a costume with a mask. The question then becomes what did they rule out in past investigations. What were the circumstances when the previous incidents occurred? What was special about that time? Is there some link between the victims then and now?' All these questions were ones Prison Officer Markham passed to him earlier on my behalf.

Frank put the golem book away, looking a little disappointed that I wanted to talk about the non-spooky explanations instead.

'I couldn't find a link between the victims. In 1809, two were convicted of the same crime – they'd killed a man to steal his money. The third was a convicted burglar. Until Officer Hyde's demise, all the previous victims were prisoners. Each death was investigated, of course, but to date no one has been convicted or even arrested. You should consider, Tempest, that the reason for that is the killer is a golem. That does mean someone is controlling it; golems do what they are instructed to do, they do not have independent thought. Finding out who controls it and why they might want Prison Officer Hyde dead is where you need to aim your efforts.'

Well, he wasn't wrong there. I still felt an unwavering concern that I was bunking with a man who snapped a prison officer in half a few hours ago. But even if I was right about Claude, someone had to be controlling him, and that worried me more.

There were other things I was curious about. 'Frank, there are cameras all over the prison, but the golem was only caught on one and only for a very brief moment.'

He grinned at me through the Perspex. 'It made the screen go fuzzy, didn't it?' He could tell by my frown he had it right. 'It's a common problem for ghost hunters and those seeking to prove the paranormal. It's also how we know all those daft supernatural *Most Haunted* programs on the television are such utter guff.'

'You've lost me.'

Frank rolled his eyes. 'It's electrostatic displacement, Tempest. I know I've said it before, but you really ought to study your own craft. Almost all supernatural beings create havoc with electrical circuits. Wizards and those who purvey magic more so than any other. A golem is essentially run on dark magical energy so of course it messes with camera feeds.'

I laughed flippantly. 'Of course. What was I thinking?'

Visiting was nearly over, and I had exhausted my list of questions. Frank hadn't told me anything useful, but he rarely did. What I got from him was food for thought and an insight into the criminal's mind. If they were using the legend of the golem to further their ambitions, they might obey certain rules.

I could only guess for now, but armed with a little more knowledge, I bade my friend goodbye and let my guards escort me back to my cell in the maximum-security wing.

Ambush

FRIDAY, MAY 12TH 1722HRS

Back in my cell, I found the ever-silent Claude still scrunched on his bunk reading the same book as before. He didn't look up when I came in, either certain it had to be his cellmate because no one else would dare disturb him, or because he just didn't care who it was. I climbed onto my own bunk and stared at the ceiling. Examining the cracks in the plaster, I thought about what I knew so far and what conclusions I could draw.

Prison Officer Hyde had been murdered. Of that there was no doubt. At this time, I had no idea why, which was a shame because knowing that might speed me to the end of the case. His death had been orchestrated to look like the work of a legendary supernatural creature. Supposedly a man made of clay, the golem left clay footprints where it walked and residue on everything it touched.

It was huge and ridiculously strong. It also had to have help to get in and out of the shower room unseen and to avoid the guards when they chased it.

Only Superintendent Yardley could sign off on doors

being operated but did that mean there was no way to do it without him knowing? I had to reserve judgement until I knew more.

Frank was able to confirm that in the original reports, the golem wore no clothes though the detail was a little patchy in both the first report and the ones that followed. No one actually said it was naked – there were very few eyewitnesses, but those who did see it mostly spoke about the glowing eyes of amber, and both the creature's size and colour. That it was made of clay came up several times.

The person or persons behind this were trying their hardest to make people believe this was a supernatural apparition that first appeared two hundred years ago, but it wasn't.

The big question, other than how on Earth I was supposed to prove any of my theories, was would it come back? Catching it was going to be tough if it never returned.

Curious to get another look at the shower room, I left my cell once more. C Wing had enough people in it that there was always some background noise. There were classes inmates could attend, the aim being to give them some basic skills that might lead to employment. They could even take more detailed courses of education that would lead to proper qualifications. Some partook, others knew they were going to be in for so long there just wasn't any point.

There were inmates at tables in the main hall of the wing. Some were reading, others were playing card games. I drew a few glances as I passed them, but no one bothered to speak to me.

The shower room was operational again. Were it not inside a prison, I'm sure the police would have shut it down for as long as they felt necessary. The badly dented basins were yet to be replaced, but otherwise it seemed back to normal and the warm moisture in the air told me it had already been used.

There had probably been an announcement about it which I missed while I was off the wing.

The killer got in here, but did he walk in through the door? The footage failed to show it, of course, the cameras going conveniently blank whenever the creature came near them. There had been no clay footprints leading into the room though, only ones leading away when it ran.

I started to poke about. That there could be a secret panel or a way into the room that no one else knew about, including the prison officers, sounded too extraordinary to consider. The golem got in somehow though.

'Well, well,' said a voice behind me.

I was standing on top of a toilet at the time, trying to reach the ceiling because I wanted to confirm to myself that it was solid. I jumped down to see how many of them there were.

The answer was a rather worrying six.

Max Travers was in the middle and it was his voice I had heard. Spread out to his left and right were men I probably recognised but couldn't place. They might be Klowns, they might be the Sandman's men; it really didn't matter.

'Henry's not here to stop us this time,' rasped Max, his hands balling into fists.

They would come soon, four or five of them rushing me while someone kept an eye on the door looking out for guards. I couldn't see any weapons, but that didn't mean they weren't carrying them.

My pulse spiked, my heart reacting to the sudden jolt of adrenaline. I had a second, not much more than that to assess my options. It was one of those occasions when I wished I had Big Ben with me.

It was just me though, and I was going to have to do the best I could.

Five rushed me before my heart could bang out its next beat. They had spread out to divide my attention, but that proved pointless because they had to converge again to get to me.

I'd come out of the toilet cubicle, but ducked back into it again, narrowing their access instantly. They hadn't considered that their angle of attack made my first move the only one available. Now they could only get to me one at a time.

Initially, at least.

Two of them crunched together, their shoulders slamming into each other as they both tried to follow me into the toilet cubicle at the same time. My hands grabbed the top of the cubicle's sides, and I lashed out with my feet, kicking both men in their faces. I was aiming for their throats, but the effect was good enough.

Wise to what they had to do, as the next one came through the opening to my front, two more scaled the toilets either side of me. The one to my front got a high elbow the second he came within striking range and I felt a sting of something on the ribs next to my left armpit as his strike went under my arm.

He fell backward when my blow landed firmly on his cheekbone, but his friends were coming over the top now and the slim advantage I gained by backing into the cubicle swung against me.

Now I was trapped.

With a snarl of anger, I spun around, reaching upward in a bid to grab a foot or an arm. If I could yank them down with enough force ... well who knows what I might have achieved because I never got the chance.

Hands came under the stall from both sides, grasping my ankles. I got no warning at all. My feet were under me one second, but not the next.

I hit my head on the way down, bringing stars and the taste of blood. I was the wrong way up, my chest to the floor as they dragged me out of the cubicle.

Things couldn't get much worse.

Trying to flip myself over, someone stamped on my right hand. It was painful enough that it brought a cry of shock from me.

Boots were going to start pummelling my ribs any second, but watching the feet to my right, suddenly a pair of them levitated.

Before my disbelieving eyes, the man floated upwards, both feet rising from the tiles at the same time.

The hands around my ankles were suddenly gone, as my attackers found something new to distract them.

No longer pinned in place, I rolled away, putting some space between me and those who wished me harm. In so doing, I saw what had caused the man to rise from the floor. I also saw that it was Max hanging in mid-air.

Claude had hold of his head.

My cellmate's giant mitt was closed around Max's skull like mine would be if I picked up a basketball. Other than that one hand, Claude wasn't touching him. My attacker dangled, making desperate noises as his neck stretched.

My eyes felt as wide as frisbees, watching to see if Claude would give Max a shake and snap his neck. I felt nothing but relief when Claude opened his hand and dropped him.

Hitting the floor, Max collapsed, then attempted to scurry away.

Claude reached out one impossibly long arm and caught Max's right foot. A second later, Max was upside down and back in the air.

I looked over to the door where they left one of their number to look out for trouble. He was laid out on the tile, flat on his back and not moving. He probably wasn't dead, I told myself, but he sure looked it.

Claude lifted his arm, the weight hanging from it of no consequence. It was as if he was lifting a box of cereal. At full stretch, Max's eyes were almost level with Claude's.

'Leave my cellmate alone,' Claude's rumbling bass voice insisted. It was the longest sentence I had heard him speak in many hours.

I could scarcely believe my eyes when he then placed Max gently back on the ground. He didn't say anything else; I guess when you are that size you don't have to.

Max ran for the door, his comrades already hustling through it with their fallen member on his feet and staggering between two as they did their best to support his weight.

I looked up at Claude.

'Thank you.'

He said, 'You're bleeding.'

Prompted to look down at myself, I spotted the bright red beginning to soak the material of my jumpsuit under my left arm. I chose that moment to lose consciousness.

Crazy Killer Behaviour... Not!

FRIDAY, MAY 12TH 2047HRS

I woke up on my bed. Attempting to sit up brought a stabbing pain under my left arm and a wave of nausea.

'One of them stabbed you,' Claude let me know. 'It's not very deep. An inch maybe. It will heal in a couple of weeks. You lost a pint or more of blood though. It hit a vein. You weren't in any danger, so I brought you back here. If I took you to sickbay, there would have been questions, then a complete search of the wing, and ... well, it wasn't bad enough to warrant the aggravation you would have suffered as a consequence.'

Though I could hear Claude, he wasn't in sight, so I rolled carefully to my left to look over the side of the bunk. He was squeezed into his bunk space as usual, reading a novel. It looked to be some trashy cozy mystery about a woman on a cruise ship. It wasn't what I expected to find an inmate reading.

'What are you in for?' I enquired, genuinely curious and not just making conversation as I popped the studs on my jumpsuit to get a look at my wound.

'Killed my wife,' he replied. 'I could tell you it was an accident, but whether it was or not really doesn't matter. In here I can harm no one else, accidentally or otherwise.'

I had a dressing where the blade, a makeshift shank no doubt, had penetrated. It was directly beneath where my arm would naturally rest, and I could remember it happening.

'You dressed my wound?' I asked, hopping gingerly down to the floor.

'Used to be a medic,' he rumbled in reply. 'I had a few bits around.' His eyes never left the page he was reading.

'Thank you.' I buttoned up my jumpsuit, observing that there was no blood on it. He'd rustled up a new one of those and put me in it too. Hardly crazy killer behaviour.

'Are you the golem?' I asked him directly.

'If I were, do you imagine I would answer truthfully?'

Fair point. I changed tack. 'You are talking. In the last minute you've said more words than the rest of the day added together. You never seem to leave the cell either. What's your deal?'

He turned the page of his book, dabbing a giant finger on his tongue first. 'I don't have a deal. I just want to be left alone. I killed my wife, I deserve to be here, but I have no wish to mingle with criminal lowlifes.'

'What happened to your last cellmate?' I was just full of questions, but I was firing some easy ones at him because I was convinced he was the golem and to prove it I was going to have to catch him out.

'He had an accident.'

A small snort of amusement left me. 'That's what Superintendent Yardley said too. Is that code for he annoyed you and you beat him to death with one of his legs?'

His eyes finally left the book, looking up to meet mine. 'Now if that were the case, it wouldn't be a great idea to annoy me with a whole bunch of questions, would it?'

Another fair point. 'I'm just trying to figure out where I stand.'

He went back to his novel. 'I am led to believe you are a good man. That is why I made sure Max Travers and his friends left you alone. I'm sorry I didn't arrive sooner.'

'I'm glad you got there when you did.'

He looked up again. 'You missed dinner. I took a bread roll for you. The guards didn't notice.' He lifted his chin, a small motion to show me where to look.

Instantly ravenous at the mention of food, I lifted what I thought was a shirt but turned out to be a pair of Claude-sized underpants. Beneath it was a dinner roll. Hardly a feast, but a lot more than nothing.

Tired from loss of blood and lack of food, I clambered back onto my bed and went to sleep.

What the Warden Wants, He Gets

SATURDAY, MAY 13TH 0610HRS

I slept soundly that night, not knowingly waking at any point before sunlight came through the small window in the cell's outer wall. Unthinkingly, I swung myself off the bed with the intention of performing half an hour or so of static exercises. Halfway through the motion, the puncture wound under my arm reminded me it was there, and I changed my mind. I could exercise tomorrow instead. Or maybe next week, I decided as I eased myself back down onto my mattress.

I don't want to say that I waited in my cell until Claude was ready to go breakfast. That's not what happened at all. That I just happened to decide to go at the same time as my giant indestructible cellmate was nothing more than coincidence and you can't prove otherwise.

I ate, ingesting my food without noticing it until my plate was suddenly clean. All the while, Max Travers, among others, glared at me. Claude was oblivious to it, focused only on his own little world. In his left hand as he powered food in with his right was another mystery novel, the dog-eared book another in the same series. I read the title: *A Sleuth and her Dachshund in Athens*. Well, at least it had a sausage dog in it. Maybe I would have a read when Claude finished it.

Prison Officer Markham found me just as I drained the last of my tea.

As ever, he had Soliman in his shadow. 'Michaels. The warden wants to see you.'

I didn't think his statement required a verbal response. I got to my feet and went with them.

Travelling through a prison takes a long time even though you don't seem to go very far. As one might expect there are a lot of doors, and protocols in place to ensure prisoners can only pass through them when they are supposed to. The doors are all electronic, the opening and closing of them managed by a person in the control room. Radios combined with cameras conveyed the requirement from one to the other as the prison officers led me through the prison.

Leaving C Wing and the hardened murderers there behind, I felt a surprising sense of relief. It was as if an invisible force bearing down on me had been removed and I was able to relax for the first time in a day.

Thirty minutes after Markham and Soliman found me at breakfast, we arrived outside the warden's office.

Soliman knocked, waited for an answer, and opened the door when called to do so.

Superintendent Yardley was inside, standing to the left of the warden's desk. The warden was behind the desk in his chair. Neither man was saying anything, and they were not looking at each other, but the tension inside that room could be cut with a knife.

They had been arguing about something. Was it me?

The golem? The warden's decision to place me in maximum-security?

A flutter of hope zipped through me as it occurred to me I might be here for the warden to rescind his decision. I didn't care about the golem case, not beyond a sense of curiosity. *Send me back to minimum-security, please.*

The warden said, 'Close the door,' the moment Markham and Soliman were inside.

Coming to a point roughly in the middle of the free space on the door side of the desk, I stopped moving and locked eyes with the prison's top man.

No one said anything.

After a two-count, the warden asked, 'Have you been able to progress, Michaels?'

Yardley's eyes were boring into the side of my head. I could feel him challenging me to tell the truth and felt a deep need to let the warden know how his top man was going out of his way to hamper me. Now was not the time though. Not with seven weeks left inside.

'I am yet to make a breakthrough, sir. There is very little to investigate.'

'How so?' the warden asked, a frown on his face.

'The golem isn't here,' I began to explain. 'He appeared and then disappeared. The cameras caught just a single glimpse of him. I'm sure you have seen the footage.'

'What about the footprints, man. What about the dead guard and all the legends? I believe you had a subject matter expert visit the jail yesterday. Have you nothing to report?'

Keeping my voice even as I might with a paying client, I told him, 'Not yet, sir. I will need more time.' I wanted to question why the warden wasn't looking harder at Claude;

the one man in the jail who matched the golem's proportions. Instead, I opted for an educated guess. 'I think this is to do with drugs, sir.'

'Drugs?' The warden couldn't understand what I was suggesting, but I wasn't watching him when I said it, my eyes were on Yardley.

I saw a muscle clench in his jaw and his eyes tightened, narrowing slightly though his surly expression never changed.

'Yes, sir, drugs. The golem is nothing more than a man dressed up to resemble a legend. Whatever might have happened here centuries ago, those are events I cannot speculate about. The current events must be motivated by something. Prison Officer Hyde's death happened for a reason. It might have been wrong place wrong time, but I think it more likely he was targeted deliberately. The witnesses all had excellent testimony to corroborate the concept that the golem is a paranormal phenomenon. However, I have interviewed enough people to know when a story has been doctored.'

The warden swung a glance toward the superintendent before bringing his eyes back to me. 'You're suggesting they didn't see the golem?'

I gave a small shake of my head. It was possible they were ordered to act, but I thought they were too convincing for that.

'I think they saw the golem, or rather, the man acting as the golem.'

The warden's eyebrows shot for the sky. 'You think it's a man?'

I shot back, 'Do you think it is an evil, animated hunk of clay?'

Yardley was on me in a heartbeat. 'You secure your tongue, Michaels!' he growled into my ear having closed the space between us.

The warden got to his feet. 'That's enough, Superintendent. I'm certain Michaels meant no disrespect.'

I flicked my eyes to meet Yardley's. If he got any closer, he was going to need to buy me a ring. Saying that was probably not in my best interest, but he was beginning to annoy me. Not least because he still fit in nicely as the bad guy behind this.

Speaking calmly, I addressed the warden again. 'Sir, I am yet to ever come across anything even remotely supernatural. The golem is a man in a costume. The clay is a prop. His glowing eyes undoubtedly an effect created with a mask and some light emitting diodes. I could make one myself in minutes after a trip to any electronics store. The question we have to ask is what was to be gained by Hyde's death.'

That the warden was disappointed to not have a supernatural mystery to solve was obvious from his face. He looked crestfallen.

'How is he getting in and out of my prison?' the warden questioned, sounding like he was trying to make a winning point.

Yardley joined in. 'Exactly, sir. There has never been an escape from this prison. Not once in over two hundred years. No one gets in or out without us knowing. Michaels is grasping at straws, sir. He clearly has no idea what he is talking about.'

Keeping my focus on the warden, I argued. 'The golem vanishes very conveniently in a passageway with cells to the left and right. None of them are occupied. How easy would it be for him to duck into one of them and come out again later?'

'Impossible,' snapped Yardley. 'That's how easy, Michaels. The cells are all controlled centrally.'

'Is each operation automatically recorded in a log or database?' I countered, adding, 'Superintendent Yardley,' at the end for good measure.

I had him, and he knew it. His lips wriggled in discomfort. I suspect he wanted to hit me.

'Is it not also the case that universal keys exist?' I was quite deliberate in not asking Yardley about his. Not yet.

Nodding my head and making a deliberate show of dismissing the head guard to turn my attention back to the warden, I delivered a line that allowed him to make the conclusion I was heading toward.

'That being the case, sir, it is not difficult to see that a person could open a cell door without anyone else knowing.'

The warden glimpsed what I was suggesting. 'So ... you think ... you're suggesting some of the prison officers are involved?'

Yardley couldn't take any more. In a flurry of movement, he gripped the front of my jumpsuit and in a single movement, lifted me off the carpet and drove backward. I could have stopped him but let him carry me back to the wall where he slammed me into it.

To my left and right, startled expressions on their faces, were Markham and Soliman. Neither man knew what to do and so did nothing, frozen to the spot with indecision.

'Stop it,' I laughed in the superintendent's face, 'You're tickling me.' He really wasn't. Just tensing my muscles was causing great discomfort around the sight of the wound under my arm.

However, my sniggering comment was enough to drive Yardley over the edge. I got a hard fist to my abdomen, though thankfully I saw it coming from a mile off. Tensing my core took most of the energy out of the blow, but there was a second one coming.

'Yardley! Enough!' roared the warden, on his feet and bright red in the face. 'I will not allow prisoner abuse!'

I locked eyes with Yardley. He had a forearm against my throat, and his weight behind it to pin me to the wall. His other arm was drawn back to deliver the second blow but paused while he fought with what he wanted to do, and the order from his boss.

That moment of doubt was all I needed.

I knew I wasn't about to employ the brightest strategy ever, but just like the decision that landed me in jail in the first place, I was going to do it anyway.

With a grin, I whispered, 'Naughty, naughty,' and as Yardley reacted, I demonstrated why putting someone against a wall isn't all that clever. Especially when they are stronger than you.

I shoved away from the wall, using a foot against the flat surface to drive the superintendent away. The moment he realised what I was doing, he dug his feet in and tried to push back.

That was exactly what I predicted he would do.

As he increased his effort, I stepped neatly to the side and swivelled off my back foot. His strength worked against him, powering him into the wall where I had been just a moment before.

Markham gasped, but if he planned to intervene, he wasn't moving fast enough to stop the leg sweep I employed to take his boss from vertical to horizontal. With our roles completely reversed, I followed Yardley down, landing with my knee pinning his hips. He was going to lash out, and to stop him I let go and thrust myself back across the room to get out of striking range.

Before I went, I gave him a wink no one else saw, and quietly murmured, 'You just overplayed your hand. You're behind this, and I'm going to catch you.'

As I was getting clear, both Markham and Soliman grabbed me. They dragged me away from the head guard but more than anything, they stopped him coming after me.

'That is enough,' the warden growled.

Yardley was back on his feet an instant later and advancing toward me. I didn't think he cared what the warden's opinion might be.

Keeping his anger in check, the superintendent growled in my face, 'You're going in the hole, Michaels. Let's see how a week in solitary works for you.'

'No.' The warden's voice cut through the room. 'He will complete his investigation.'

Yardley couldn't believe his ears. 'He just assaulted a prison officer, sir!'

'You assaulted him first, Superintendent.' Yardley opened his mouth to argue, only to have the warden cut him off. 'That is final, Yardley.' Dismissing his senior prison officer, the warden addressed the two guards holding my arms. 'Take Michaels back to C Wing. Michaels,' he shifted his gaze to meet mine, 'there are no dirty guards in this prison. Is that clear? I want you to find out what the golem is and what has caused it to manifest again at this time. I do not for one second believe it is a man in a costume and you are not getting out of maximum-security until you solve this mystery.'

I kept my mouth shut while the warden spoke, delivering a sentence that was far worse than a week in solitary. It was still shut when Markham and Soliman escorted me from the warden's office.

Walking down the corridor, I couldn't help but feel that things were only going to get worse.

Snitches Get Stitches

SATURDAY, MAY 13TH 0917HRS

My guards were silent most of the way back through the prison, but as we neared C Wing, Prison Officer Markham could hold his tongue no longer.

'You really think there could be guards involved in Hyde's murder?'

They were both behind me, and I didn't bother to turn around when I replied, 'How did the golem get in and out of the prison multiple times? How did he enter a passageway and never come out the other end? If we dismiss the notion that he is a supernatural manifestation and thus able to defy the laws of this planet, then either someone is opening doors for him, or someone is doctoring the camera footage. Whichever it is, the prisoners are not doing it. That leaves …'

'The guards,' Markham filled in the blank space I left for him and lapsed back into silence.

It was only when we came through the final gate and back into C Wing that I spoke again.

'Can you arrange for me to speak with the witnesses again, please?'

I'd been running different ideas through my head, trying to work out how I could get some kind of handle on this case. I was certain there was someone inside the maximum-security wing who was benefitting from the golem's appearance. The good money was on Henry Featherstone – the *guvnor*. I abridged the word and said it with a dirty, cockney accent in my head because it felt right to do so. He controlled the drug trade in and out, but was this about drugs? Or did I have that part wrong?

Calling Amanda or Jane and getting them to look into Prison Officer Hyde's past might yield what he was up to, but I was going to do this without involving my friends on the outside if I could.

I still suspected Yardley. He was the one hampering my attempts to investigate, and according to Markham, he was the only person able to authorise cell doors being opened and closed outside of normal operations. Would anyone question him if he went into the control room and fiddled with something?

Probably not. And it wouldn't show up on a log anywhere because the system was too old for that.

When I got to speak with Spider Murphy, Kev the Knuckle, and the others the first time, Yardley had been right there. I remember them glancing across the room, but I hadn't paid enough attention to see whether the senior guard was controlling what they said and giving them a warning glare.

Maybe if I could get them alone again now, I could wheedle out of them what they actually saw.

To my request, Markham said, 'I'll see what I can do.'

Soliman revolted. 'What? You're going to help him? He's trying to prove the guards are dirty!'

'But what if they are?' countered Markham, trying to get his partner to see sense. 'What if Michaels is bang on the money and there is someone in the guards behind Hyde's death? What if it's Yardley? Would we know if he was sneaking a person in here? Would we know if he was working with Featherstone?'

'He can't be,' argued Soliman, but he didn't sound too sure of himself.

They delivered me back to my cell, Markham promising he would do what he could to organise somewhere for me to speak in private to the inmates in question.

Claude was on his bunk, reading as usual. He looked up as I came in.

'How is your wound?'

I suspected it was worse after the tussle with Yardley, but it would recover, and it wasn't worth mentioning my discomfort to Claude.

'It's much better than it would be without your help,' I let him know.

He gave a head tilt of acknowledgement and went back to his book.

Lunch came and went, the food filling my belly though, like breakfast, I paid little attention to it. I was looking around for Markham and Soliman. They were supposed to be getting me a place to talk to Spider Murphy and the other witnesses yet there was no sign of them.

I could see Spider, his awful tattoo easy to pick out. I wanted to go over and speak to him, but when I began to rise from my seat, I felt my blood run cold.

Sitting opposite Spider with his back to me was a man I

had never expected to see again. I knew him as Harry Hengist though his real name was Ramsey Mitchell. A serial killer known as the Sandman, I had been a key element in his capture, and he knew it.

Staring at the back of his head, I guess someone said something to him because he twisted in his seat to look over at me. I got a smile and a wave.

I'm not ashamed to admit I felt my stomach tighten and the meal I'd just eaten threatened to revolt. The only comfort I felt was the giant form of Claude sitting next to me, one hand holding his book, the other gripping a burger he was halfway through eating.

Were it not for him, I might have died yesterday in the shower room. Unfortunately, I couldn't shift the belief that he was the golem.

How do I find myself in these situations?

A little voice at the back of my head suggested it might be a good time to call Amanda and my parents. I was supposed to be serving an eight week stretch in minimum-security. I came into the prison intending to work on my one rep max bench press and trim down my waist. Instead, I was beginning to calculate the odds of making it out alive.

I asked a question.

'Claude, how often do inmates get killed in here?'

Claude turned his page, acting as if he hadn't heard me and I was about to ask again when he got to the end of a paragraph and looked up.

'Never. Well, I guess that's not true because it has happened in the past, but I think it has been years since an inmate was killed in an altercation. Injuries, yes, not that any are ever traced back to the person responsible. Inmates don't snitch. Golden rule, that one.'

'Yeah.' None of this was doing my pulse any favours. It

was due to be exercise hour shortly, a brief excursion into the daylight and fresh air in the yard outside. Maybe I would be able to get close to Kev the Knuckle; he didn't appear to be keeping company with the Sandman and his goons.

I didn't get to the yard.

Stripped Bare

SATURDAY, MAY 13TH 1354HRS

The crowd in the kitchen area slowly dissipated, the guards sending the inmates back to their tasks if they had them, or off to the leisure area if they were permitted.

The call for exercise came just before 1400hrs, a message over the address system telling everyone to make their way to the centre of the wing where we were lined up each day.

Coming out of my cell, I had Claude ahead of me, his giant form filling the passageway. A flight of stairs, the steel mesh kind you can see through, would take us down to the floor below where inmates were already beginning to gather.

My eyes were on the crowd below, picking out the people I wanted to speak to. It would be conspicuous to do so in the open of the yard, so I needed to be behind Spider or Kev if I wanted to talk to them on the way out. Of course, I could only do that provided they were not already right next to the Sandman or someone else who wanted dearly to gut me like a fish.

Had my focus been on the stairs and what was happening in my immediate vicinity, I might have noticed the warning signs and been able to stop what happened next.

As it was, the first thing I heard was a gasp from Claude as he fell. There was something across the top of the stairs, I caught a glimpse of it being hastily removed when my head and eyes snapped around.

Claude fell, his arms pinwheeling and looking for purchase. He would have been able to grab hold of something had it not been for another inmate who was on the stairs just ahead of him.

That man, not one I knew, but who caught my eye as he glanced up at me, knocked Claude's hand away as he tried to grab the railing. No one else would have seen it, only me; Claude's tumble had been well choreographed.

He pitched into free air, falling headfirst and unable to stop himself.

I surged after him, but there was nothing I could do to prevent the inevitable crash as he hit the floor below.

A crunching sound echoed across the whole wing, accentuated by shouts from the prison officers as they attempted to keep the inmates where they were while also running to Claude's aid themselves.

I barged by the man I'd seen knock Claude's arm aside. I wanted to deal with him but doing so now would be seen as an act of aggression that probably would get me a spell in solitary. I memorised his face as I flew down the steps.

Before I could get to the bottom, Superintendent Yardley stepped out to block my path.

'Whoa there, Michaels. Stop where you are. Did you just push that inmate?'

I scrunched up my face. Was Yardley behind this?

'I tripped,' Claude managed to blurt between pain-filled gasps. 'Lost my footing is all that happened, sir.'

Yardley never took his eyes off me. 'Are you injured, Claude?'

Claude was trying to get up. 'I'll be fine, sir. Just a few bruises.'

The superintendent pursed his lips and frowned. 'Best we take you to sickbay and get you checked out. You can spend a night in there where we can monitor you and make sure you didn't do any damage that is yet to present itself. That looks like a nasty bump on your head. Can't be too careful. You could be concussed.'

I sniffed in a deep breath, filling my lungs, but not saying a word. Yardley was running the show, dictating terms and playing things the way he wanted to. I'd challenged him openly in the warden's office, telling him I knew he was behind it all. Now he was removing Claude, the one person who had provided me with a semblance of safety. Claude probably was hurt, but not badly. I would be without him now though and if the Sandman, Max Travers, or anyone else came for me, I would be completely alone.

Then another thought occurred to me, one equally as disquieting as the previous. If Claude was in the sickbay, how hard would it be for Yardley to have him act as the golem again? Was that the plan? Was there a reason he needed the golem in play, or was it just so the golem could be the one to kill me?

A memory of Hyde's broken body flashed through my head, making my stomach churn unpleasantly.

Yardley stepped away, clapping his hands. 'Yard time is going to waste! Get these inmates outside!'

'Where's Markham and Soliman?' I called to the superintendent's retreating back.

He turned halfway around but kept walking away. 'Reassigned, Michaels. Reassigned.' He clicked his fingers at another prison officer. 'Michaels failed to address me respectfully. Remove his telephone privileges for a week.'

The prison officer looked my way. 'Yes, sir.'

I was stripped bare. Anyone who might have helped was now out of reach. Falling in with the procession of prisoners going outside, I felt numb.

The Top of the Pile

SATURDAY, MAY 13TH 1416HRS

It's no exaggeration to say I felt low as I trudged around the yard. The warden wasn't going to let me out until I had solved the case and either produced the golem or unequivocal proof that it was a hoax. The latter required me to work out who was behind it, why, and how, and then get that information to the warden.

Maybe the warden would summon me again for an update tomorrow, but was I going to survive the night? Who could I turn to?

Half a dozen times, inmates shoulder barged me as I wandered the yard. It wasn't intended to hurt me, just remind me that I was on my own.

The small form of Henry Featherstone appeared before me.

'Mr Michaels, you appear to be out of favour,' he observed.

It felt like a statement about my state of mind that I couldn't come up with a flippant response.

'With so many enemies seeking your demise, I fear there

is only so much I can do for you, Mr Michaels. Are you any closer to solving the mystery? The golem will strike again.'

I frowned at his statement. 'Why do you say that? What do you know?'

'Know, Michaels? I know the code. Speaking up if I knew who was behind this would place me in the same category as say … a private investigator who put half the residents in here.'

A tired snort of laughter shook my shoulders at his choice of comparison.

'You can't tell me anything, because this is about the movement of drugs and admitting what you know would be tantamount to admitting your involvement,' I concluded, holding his gaze as I accused him.

A smile played across the smaller man's lips and I felt a presence behind me.

'Do I need to teach him some manners, boss?' asked Harker.

'Yeah, boss, this one has an attitude,' added Bowman.

I tensed myself, questioning whether getting locked in solitary might save me from a worse fate. If either man twitched, we were going to find out.

Henry held my gaze for another second before giving his henchmen a small head shake.

'Mr Michaels is entitled to voice his thoughts.' He turned and started to walk away.

'Who's behind the golem, Henry?' I called out, my voice raised. 'Tell me who it is!'

Henry Featherstone, apex prisoner, just kept walking. Over his shoulder he told me, 'You are looking in the wrong place, Mr Michaels.'

I tried to follow him only to find my path blocked by two men roughly the size and shape of refrigerators. Harker and Bowman glared at me, challenging me to try something.

I returned their hard stares, still calculating whether I stood to gain overall by starting a fight. I might have gone for it were it not for the distinct possibility that whoever was letting the golem move around the prison might also let it into solitary.

Featherstone was gone, merged with the crowd. If he didn't want to talk to me, I wasn't going to get to ask him any more questions. But he'd given me a steer even if he didn't mean to. He wanted me to find the golem, which had to mean he was worried it might cause him a problem.

Or it already was.

When Spider Murphy came within speaking distance, I was too lost inside my own head to bother asking him any questions. Did his testimony matter anymore though? What Featherstone said had stuck with me. If I took his statement at face value, then it changed my approach to the case. He had influence, but if he was controlling the flow of contraband into the prison, then his biggest challenge had to be maintaining his position.

Wasn't that true of everyone at the top of every mountain – new challengers would always come along. Was there someone new taking a bite out of Henry's empire?

The golem appeared several times before it killed Hyde. Why?

As a warning? I tried that idea on for size.

As we filed back inside under the watchful eyes of the prison guards, I knew my time was probably short if I wanted to figure this out.

I could not have been more right.

Late Night Rescue?

SATURDAY, MAY 13TH 2349HRS

I spent most of the rest of the day sitting with my back against the wall in the central area of the wing. I wanted to be in plain sight where I could see people coming and always had at least one prison officer in my sight.

No one bothered me; however, I saw plenty of inmates glance my way or openly observe me from across the room while chatting with one or more of their colleagues. Whatever they had planned, it was set to happen later.

It crossed my mind to make a shank, yet it felt like a step in the wrong direction. My pulse was high most of the time, the potential for what might happen continually invading my thoughts as I tried different scenarios for the golem and who might be behind it.

At dinner time, I made sure I was at the head of the queue and once I'd eaten, I asked a guard to lock my cell. He was surprised by the request but called it in, getting someone in the control room to lock it once I was inside.

Did that make me feel safer? Not really, but safety wasn't the driver behind my request. Going around and around in my head were questions about Yardley. He'd been hampering me since the start and wasted no time in making sure Claude was out of reach today. He was the one with a universal key. He had the power and influence inside the prison to do as he pleased. Was he the one now challenging Henry Featherstone's grip on the drug trade?

When I whispered to him that I knew he was behind it, I foolishly tipped my hand. Now I was going to be the next victim of the golem, I felt sure of it. Yardley's only choice was to silence me before I had a chance to prove what I believed.

I've fought bigger men. I've fought more than one at a time. Rarely for real though, it was always in sparring sessions in a dojo somewhere, and the fight was intended as a hypothetical lesson. Whatever I might have done in practice or real life in the past, Claude was on a different spectrum. Immensely strong, hugely tall, with a wingspan that had to be close to three metres. Heck, maybe it was more than that.

To fight a person like that, it was no good attempting to stay outside of his reach, I had to get inside it where I could do damage yet avoid him getting hold of me.

It was still light outside and would stay that way until some point after nine o'clock. Convinced I was safe until the inmates were all locked up and in bed for the night, I set my mental alarm clock – a trick that developed through many years in the army – and went to sleep.

When I awoke a few hours later, I was relieved to know that I had guessed right. It was just getting dark outside and the sounds of movement and chatter inside the prison were all but gone. The golem hadn't come for me yet, but it would soon.

It happened at close to midnight, the unmistakable

sound of the lock on my cell door popping open. It jarred me from my semi-alert state with a surge of adrenaline. I came to my feet, sliding across the narrow cell to hug the wall where I then went into a crouch.

Whoever came through the door was going to get a serious smack in the trousers and maybe I would get to test out my theory about Claude and his bowling balls.

Mercifully, the person coming through the door had the sense to speak first.

'Michaels,' hissed Prison Officer Markham. 'Michaels.' He was coming into the cell at a normal pace, expecting to find me in my bed.

When I stood up and spoke right next to his ear, he squealed like a little girl and jumped across the cell to bounce off the far wall.

'Michaels! What the hell are you doing?' He clutched at his chest and gasped for breath. 'You scared the life out of me.'

Ignoring his question, I asked one of my own. 'What's going on?'

Markham sucked in a deep breath. 'There's been another golem sighting, and it looks like you might have been right about Claude. He's broken out of sickbay. There're two dead already - Harker and Bowman.'

My eyes flared at the news though I shouldn't have found it surprising to hear. This confirmed my theories about what was happening. 'Featherstone's henchmen? Where is he now?'

Markham started back out of my cell door. 'Your guess is as good as mine, Michaels. Somewhere inside the prison.'

He was back outside in the corridor, but my feet weren't moving to follow him. 'Why did you come for me?' I asked, a frown creasing my forehead.

My question caused Markham to choke. 'Isn't it obvious? If Claude is the golem and Yardley is behind it, he is going to want you out of the way. You won't be safe in your cell.'

I found my feet moving, taking me out of my cell and along the corridor toward the stairs Claude fell down earlier. My brain wasn't connected to them; it was processing the new information and trying to make sense of it. The wing was dark, the only light supplied by the moon as it shone through the windows. At night the prison was locked down, the inmates all tucked up safely in their beds. There was no need for lights to be on because no one would be moving around, just an occasional patrol.

However, the inmates of C Wing were awake in their cells, I could hear them talking, discussing what they could hear in the corridor outside.

I hurried past them. At the top of the stairs, I asked, 'Where are we going?'

'Out of here,' Markham waved for me to follow, urgent gestures to suggest dawdling might cost me dearly.

'How?' I wanted to know, my pace slowing again as we descended into the kitchen area. 'Where is Soliman? The prison officers never travel alone; there are always two of you. And if Yardley is behind this, Control won't open the doors to let me out of C Wing.'

'Soliman is just ahead, Michaels,' insisted Markham, getting annoyed at my reluctance to follow him, 'and I have Yardley's master key. I swiped it earlier, that's how we are going to get you out. I'll take you to the warden; you can tell him about your suspicions.'

My feet stopped again. 'You said it couldn't possibly be Claude. You were adamant about it.'

Markham gave an exaggerated gesture of exasperation.

'Actually, Soliman said that, not me. And I guess he was wrong.'

I chewed my lip for a second. Yesterday I made a comment about Yardley having a universal key and that it could account for the golem vanishing, but I hadn't expressed to Markham my suspicions about the head guard.

Understanding hit my brain like an electric shock.

'Michaels we have to go!' hissed Markham.

He reached one of his big ham fists to grab me. I danced back a foot, keeping some distance between us. 'Why did you volunteer to be my chaperone?'

Markham tried to grab my arm again; he wanted to go and was ready to make me accompany him. I slapped his hand away and snorted a small sigh of tired self-deprecating laughter.

'It's you, isn't it? You're doing what? Moving in on the drug trade? You plan to take over the whole operation. Did you kill Yardley to get the key?'

'What? Why would it be ...' Markham started to argue, before stopping himself mid-sentence. 'Aw, heck, why bother. Yes, Michaels. I've worked for Henry Featherstone for years. First as an enforcer - size has its advantages – then, when he got incarcerated here, I was expected to get a job here and help him move his product. Well, I'm moving up in the world and Henry Featherstone is moving into a grave. He set me up nicely and taught me everything I need to know.'

I tilted my head over to the right until it clicked. Then to the left. I softened my posture, making my legs loose and flexed so they were ready to move, and I brought my arms up ready.

'You think we are going to fight?' Markham scoffed.

I was giving away a hundred pounds and over half a

foot in height. If he got hold of me, he might be able to squeeze me until my ribs popped, but we were going to find out.

Or so I thought.

Just as I was about to launch myself at him – planning to get my defence in early by attacking first, I saw his focus shift. His eyes left my face and swung upward. Then upward some more and a creeping sensation rode up my spine to make my hair stand on end.

My shoulders slumped a little in defeat when I saw Markham's eyes come back to mine with a smile attached.

I sighed, 'The golem is behind me, isn't it?'

Face to Face with a Golem

SATURDAY, MAY 13TH 2358HRS

I spun around. I hadn't heard it approach; maybe clay feet make no noise, but there it was. Even knowing it was a man inside the clay, I couldn't help the fear that shot through me when its eyes flicked open to reveal two burning orange coals. It was huge, just as big in real life as it looked in the picture and I could see where the clay had been moulded to it.

My heart was in my throat. I hadn't been this desperate to run away since I faced what turned out to be a surgically enhanced polar bear in the Alps. I escaped that time because I was on a slope and able to turn myself into a human toboggan.

No such escape route was going to present itself this time. I was in the mess hall area surrounded by tables and chairs. They might be useful as weapons but that would apply to everyone in the fight.

Markham sounded thoroughly amused when he said, 'I have to hand it to you, Michaels. If I'd left it another day, I think you would have worked it out for yourself. It's a shame really, we might have been pals if you weren't such a boy scout.'

'You were wrestlers?' I guessed. 'A tag-team or something.'

Markham made an impressed noise though the golem didn't twitch. I couldn't even tell if it was breathing.

'That's exactly what I mean, Michaels. You have this knack for seeing the answers. Yes, the golem and I have known each other for a long time. When our wrestling career petered out, we found work with Henry Featherstone, breaking arms and such. It was never going to make me rich though, so I came up with a new plan: taking over the drug trade in here, just as you guessed. The golem is going to remove all my opposition and then cease to exist again. First though, it is going to kill you.'

The golem surged forward, a huge hulking mass of lumbering muscle. I had Markham to my rear, a more dangerous sandwich than I had ever been in before, but where they are both big, they are also slow. Slower than me at least.

I shot to my right, changing the angles so they were both coming at me from the same direction.

'Claude!' I yelled. 'Claude, you don't have to be this person. You don't have to kill for him!'

My cellmate had been so reasonable and quiet. He read mystery novels and kept to himself. Had he really killed his wife, or was he just a good actor?

They ran at me, both of them. I was faster, but even though we were in one of the wing's main open spaces, the pair of them would narrow the angles and pin me eventually. Trying to evade them was a tactic that would fail sooner or later.

Sooner, it turned out, when I leapt a table in a classic Parkour move. I intended to get the table between me and Markham, thus slowing him down, but the rogue guard whacked the table with one massive arm, bowling it down the hall.

I had to dive out of its way, losing valuable seconds as I scrambled back to my feet. Markham was closing on me and the golem was right in my way. Markham had learned from his trick with the table and now had a chair in each hand.

I was about to lose.

So I did the dumbest thing I could think of – I attacked the golem. With two fast steps, I ran up a chair, onto a table and launched myself into the air.

A chair slammed into the table as I leapt off it, clattering away into the shadows.

The superman punch, when correctly executed, can end a fight. The practitioner converts their potential energy in the air to deliver a blow many times stronger than one can create in a static position.

At the apex of my leap, I was just about high enough that I was going to punch downward to the golem's face. I threw my lead leg backward, creating a pendulum effect as my striking arm arced forward.

The golem swatted me to the side like I was a fly.

My fist actually connected with his face first, but his strike to my side, like being hit with a telegraph pole, ensured I got only a glancing blow and the energy in it was lost to the air.

My breath flew from me as I tumbled, messages reporting in from my ribs to let me know I was in trouble before the rest of me found a table to collide with.

I bounced off that, took a chair with me as I spun out of

control, and came to rest in a tangle of limbs. I could taste blood and was struggling to breathe.

Feet were coming my way – Markham's boots moving fast to get to me, and the golem's giant clay covered feet.

I tried to roll onto my front, needing to get my arms under my body so I could get up, but the first attempt failed, my arms failing to respond to my commands swiftly enough.

There was no time for a second attempt.

The golem got to me first, just as I managed to get my body flipped the right way. He reached down with a giant right hand, coming for my neck.

I kicked at it, ignoring the pain in my ribs and back and hips, and the dancing lights in front of my eyes. The first blow connected, kicking his hand away, but the golem put a knee on the floor, brought his left arm into play as well, and had me pinned in a second.

Then he lifted me from the floor by my neck. My teeth were gritted hard, my fingers digging at his hand as he slowly squeezed the life from me.

As the fuzziness in my head began to take over and the shadow-filled room started to dim, I heard myself, wheeze, 'Claude.'

Then the sound of something wooden smashing reached my ears and I tumbled to the floor again.

Landing with both feet only to crumple like a house of cards, I coughed and choked and looked about in complete confusion.

The golem and Markham were no longer looking my way; they were staring at a new foe. One who I had been wrong about from the start.

Seeing him face off against a pair of killers, a smile

twisted my lips and new hope buoyed me from the floor and back onto my feet.

He aimed a nod my way as he squared off against Markham and the golem.

I gave him one back with a word of acknowledgement, 'Claude.'

Two Golems?

SUNDAY, MAY 14TH 0002HRS

Claude's naked form was covered in clay just like the real one and needed only a mask on his head to complete the transformation. It confused me for a second, my brain struggling to comprehend what I was seeing.

There were two golems?

No, that wasn't it. They were going to frame him for the murders! He would be found covered in clay and no jury would believe he wasn't guilty. It was neat, but the fact that he was here and had just saved me was enough to convince me he wasn't on their side.

That there were two men of equally huge height and stature in the same place defied belief, yet here they were. I had no idea as to Claude's ability as a fighter. He'd most likely never needed to find out - guys that size don't get many challengers. We were about to find out if he could hold his own though. Gentle giant or not, he was in a fight to the death now.

Markham told me Claude escaped sickbay, but that wasn't going to be true.

Claude had the remains of a chair in his hands, just a couple of legs were all that remained but with a tug of satisfaction I saw the golem reach up to touch its head – it was bleeding. Where Claude had hit it, the blow had scraped off the clay and cut its scalp.

'Hey, Markham!' I called to draw his attention. Then I punched him in the throat when his face turned my way and dropped into a leg sweep that sent him to the floor.

With moonlight streaming through the windows far above, the C Wing mess hall was all shadows and dark corners, but we were right in the middle, illuminated like actors on a dark and deadly stage as the four of us faced off.

No one was coming to rescue me. But maybe at the very least we could do enough damage that the golem wouldn't escape. Surely someone would be coming to check on the wing shortly. Surely there were cameras in the control room that someone would see.

But then, how many of the guards worked for Markham? As he made his play to take over the prison and its product distribution, had he recruited enough of the guards to ensure he could kill in plain sight yet never be caught?

Was Yardley involved? Had he given Markham the master key or was he already dead? I had to force the flood of questions from my mind, clearing it so I could figure out a strategy better than getting into a street brawl with a couple of wrestlers.

Too late, the golem roared in rage and ran at Claude. Markham saw my eyes twitch to see what happened and chose that moment to surge at me. I was still hurting badly and moving sluggishly from being thrown across the room. Had I not been, I might have tried to finish Markham when I got him down. A sleeper hold might have done it, but given his strength, size, and wrestling ability, the possibility that he would have converted my hold into a winning one for himself was all too great.

The last thing I wanted was to let him get hold of me.

However, my mixed martial arts background has some Judo and Aikido in it, so when Markham lanced out a hand, not to punch me, but to grab my jumpsuit, I gripped his hand with both of mine, put my elbows high so he couldn't easily hit my face and twisted with all my might.

The bones in our bodies only go one way for the most part. Force them to bend in a direction they don't like, and pain is instant.

Markham yelled and tried to yank his hand back. I held it for a nanosecond, then shoved it away just as he increased his effort. He fell backward and slid a yard along the floor. It gave me space.

And I used it.

I ran toward Claude and the golem, throwing myself at the floor so I slid on my butt.

The golem had Claude by his neck, and I got to see a terrible headbutt smash into Claude's face before I could stop it.

Arriving behind the golem, I kicked up behind his knees, felling him like a tree.

Claude reeled back as the golem fell away, his face was covered in blood, his nose spread across his face, and his right eye was all but swollen shut. On top of that, his left shoulder hung awkwardly as if dislocated and I suspected that was exactly what I was seeing.

We were not going to win this fight. One could say it was already lost. Hanging around would just get us killed, so I grabbed Claude's good arm and started running.

Both our opponents were down, but as I took the first step away from them, I changed my mind.

A plan had popped into my head. It was quite honestly insane, but I was going to do it anyway.

Crazy Plans

SUNDAY, MAY 14TH 0011HRS

Letting go of Claude's arm, I shoved him toward the far side of the mess hall and toward the main hall in the middle of C Wing – the exit was that direction.

When I turned around again, I saw the golem getting back to his feet. I ran at him, grabbing a chair with my right hand. It was right there for me to use, and the relative distances were perfect. I snatched hold of the head of the chair in one hand, whipped it in a tight arc and exploded it on the golem's face.

He went down again. It even drew a cry of pain, and I might have allowed myself a fist bump if I didn't still think we were probably going to die.

Markham was getting to his feet, but was still on his knees, winded from the impact of hitting the floor. Not only that, he was facing away from me. I tackled him like it was a game of rugby just as he started to stand.

He went down hard beneath me, and I questioned whether I could employ the sleeper hold like he had on a prisoner a couple of days ago. Taking out one of the pair would increase our odds significantly. However, a quick glance at the golem told me how bad of an idea that would be.

My use of the chair had cut him again. He was bleeding from his mouth and a cut on his left cheekbone. The chair had even knocked out one of the orange lights in his mask which was now torn to reveal the white flesh beneath. However, the injuries and damage had done nothing to dissuade him from getting back in the fight.

He was coming for me, scrambling to get off the floor, so with Markham briefly pinned beneath me, I felt for the thing I needed, yanked it free and did my best impression of the Road Runner.

Claude had already staggered to the other side of the mess hall though I could see behind the pain in his eyes, confusion about what we were supposed to do now. We couldn't open the door there to get through to the wing's main hall, so we were trapped.

Except I didn't think we were.

Markham boasted about having a universal key. Well, he didn't have it any more.

I slammed into the gate next to Claude, heart pumping hard in my chest as I tried the electronic key. If he had been lying about it, we would be in big trouble.

With a surge of hope, I heard the solenoid click, and the gate swung free.

Behind us, Markham screamed his rage, flailing at his waist where the key had hung until I relieved him of it. He hadn't realised that was my intention.

Roaring, 'Get him, you idiot!' at the golem, Markham ran at me.

With a shove, I got Claude through the gate and shut it

again mere fractions of a second before Markham and the golem reached it.

Safe behind the steel bars of the gate, I sucked in a few deep breaths.

The golem gripped the bars and shook them, wrenching the gate this way and that but to no avail. The gate was built to withstand greater forces than even he could generate.

I'd been holding my breath as he yanked at it, envisaging a comedy moment from a cartoon where he would rip the whole thing from its mooring points in the ancient brickwork.

Now imbued with some confidence, I faced Markham once more.

'What was the plan? Frame Claude as the golem?'

'I woke up like this,' Claude indicated the clay on his body. 'I think they put something in my food because I don't remember anything after dinner. It was obvious then that they planned to frame me for Hyde's death.'

Glaring at Markham through the bars, I said, 'They killed Harker and Bowman tonight too. Who was next?' I asked. 'Featherstone?'

'Naturally,' Markham didn't care about revealing his plan now, which should have acted as a warning to me, but it didn't. I was still telling myself we were safe behind the bars.

'I saw it,' wheezed Claude from behind me, wincing as he shifted position.

Seeing the pain displayed on his face, I tore off the sleeves of my jumpsuit, and while he talked, I fashioned a sling to support his injured arm.

'It was across the prison. I could see it through the window as he let it in,' Claude nodded his head toward Markham, removing any ambiguity as to who *him* might be.

'The sickbay overlooks C Wing,' Claude explained. 'I tried to get someone's attention but the guard who should have come when I shouted never appeared, and when I checked it, I found the door to sickbay had been left open. I saw the golem go into Bowman's cell.'

'Taking out the competition,' I nodded my head, seeing Markham's grand plan for what it was. 'Rule by fear and force.'

Markham, still acting like he could win, smiled at me. 'It doesn't matter if the inmates believe in the golem as long as they believe it will kill them when they fail to obey the rules.'

'Your rules,' I pointed out.

I got a nod. 'Yes, Michaels. This prison is a fully functioning microsystem. There is money to be made here for the man at the top and it's a totally safe environment in which to do it because there can be no competition.'

'Not once Featherstone has been removed,' I concluded.

Markham gave me a half shrug to show that he sort of agreed. 'Featherstone and others.'

'What did Hyde do?' I wanted to know, but I gave him my best guess first. 'He wouldn't play ball, would he? You have enough of the guards in your pocket, but he was going to blow the whistle.'

I got the appreciative look again. 'Like I said before, Michaels, you have a keen ability to work things out. That's why I volunteered to handle you when Yardley asked. I was hoping you would poke around and then go back to minimum-security. Alas, you insisted on digging. Now you must die before you can talk to anyone.'

I hitched an eyebrow, looking at the solid steel gate that kept us apart.

'How are you planning to manage that?'

With an amused twinkle in his eye that shot a blast of ice through my veins, Markham lifted his radio.

Shouting in a panicked voice, he yelled, 'Control there are prisoners escaping! Michaels is on the loose. There are two dead! I think he might have killed them. It looks like Monet is the golem and Michaels is working with him! Send help quickly and open the door between the kitchen and the main hall in C Wing! I am going to try to corral them!'

I said a bad word and my eyes flared in panic. The next door was two yards away, the space between acting sort of like an air lock to limit prisoner movement and minimise how far they could get if they ever did get through a door.

I darted to it, shoving Claude ahead of me. With desperate fingers, I pressed the universal key to the lock just as the solenoid on the previous gate operated again.

Claude and I fell through the gap just as Markham and the golem came through the gate behind us and I threw the second gate shut.

'Claude, we have to go!' I wanted to run, but I wasn't going to leave him behind. He was the only reason I was still alive, and he saved my life twice now. However, my cellmate was a slow-moving object, even with me towing him.

Markham was on his radio again, calling to whoever he had in his pocket in the control room. They would have that second door open in a second and they would catch us before we made it to the next one unless we did something crazy.

Remember that daft plan I had?

I didn't have the time to spare, but after running to the next gate, I ran to the wall just the other side. Common sense dictated we keep moving; only by keeping at least one barrier between us could we survive, but I'd been looking for something since I worked out Markham was controlling a large portion of the prison officers, and there it was, on the wall.

With a satisfied grin, I punched the fire alarm.

The wail of the alarm was instant, filling the air with its high-pitched and insistent notes.

That was going to get someone's attention.

Markham came through the gate behind us, a seething look of hatred etched on his brow. He wanted to kill me good now.

'A fire locks down all the doors, right? No one can move now, but whoever is running the control room — I assume that isn't someone in your pocket — will have to send all the prison officers to fight the fire and ensure prisoner safety.' With a smug grin, I said, 'Game, set, match, me.'

The golem came up to the bars again, its teeth showing and its fists balling. It wanted to tear something apart, yet we were beyond reach on the other side of a steel barrier.

I allowed myself a deep shudder as I relaxed. We were safe. The guards would come, the warden too, no doubt, and I could tell him all there was to tell.

So why didn't Markham look worried.

This time he lifted a phone to his lips. 'Soliman, it's Markham. Open all the doors in C Wing.'

A muffled exclamation came back over his radio.

'Just do it. There is no fire. Open everything. I want a full riot. Let's see if Michaels can escape through an entire prison of enemies.'

Enemies Everywhere

SUNDAY, MAY 14TH 0013HRS

I'll admit my stomach tightened as his words reached my brain. All the doors were going to open. All of them including the one I was looking through right now. Not only that, Markham had Soliman inside the control room and that meant he could set all the inmates free.

Did I have two seconds or ten?

I'd lost two seconds frozen to the spot as blind panic set in.

The sound of the electronic lock shifting on multiple cell doors filled the air. The inmates were being released. How Markham expected to get away with this was a moot point if I was dead, which I most certainly would be if the Sandman and his acolytes, or the Klowns caught me.

Still frozen to the spot, my breath coming in heaving fearful lumps, I was jolted back into motion when the door to my front popped open. I grabbed for it at the same time as the golem.

I got there first, but rather than attempt to keep it shut, a pointless gesture I felt sure, I yanked it open. The golem's hands hit free air and came through the opening gap, whereupon I slammed the gate shut again.

His fingers, fat sausage like digits that they are, were nevertheless made from flesh and blood and they stood no chance against half inch thick steel bar.

The golem screamed with pain as I crushed, mangled, and cut his fingers with one blow. He fell back, and with my weight keeping the door shut, I used the universal card to lock it again.

I had no idea if that would work, but when the door buzzed and locked, it did so to an angry bellow from Markham.

I'd bought us a few seconds – he would get the door open again soon enough, but my bigger problem was the sound of prisoner footsteps on the steel mesh stairs. They were coming, and even though there were some who had no beef with me, they would do nothing to stop those who planned to skin me alive.

It was well past time to run.

Shoving Claude ahead of me, we dashed across the main hall.

A shout from above let me know I'd already been spotted.

I looked up to see the Sandman smiling down at me from the landing above. My sense of impending doom went up a notch.

'Claude, we have to go, buddy! If we don't get to the exit door and lock it again, these guys will be all over the prison. Lives will get lost.'

I got a rumble of reply from my oversized friend. He knew the stakes. He also knew the likelihood of me surviving if we didn't get to the door. It was slim to say the least.

Pouring down the stairs, directed by the Sandman and thus almost certainly a wave of his followers, came a dozen men from my right.

Claude and I were running down the middle of the wing's main hall, the exit gate right ahead of us. The inmates hadn't worked out it was open yet, which was both good and bad. It meant we might prevent them from escaping the wing itself – they would be easier to manage if all contained in one place, but also bad because it meant they were all focused on me.

A glance behind showed Markham and the golem nowhere in sight. They had gone another way, Markham choosing to keep his monster secret. Plus, he only wanted me dead, I don't think he cared how it happened.

It was one less thing to worry about but hardly comforting.

From my left came a different bunch, Max Travers among them – the Klowns.

I was hip-deep in lowlife scumbags. The ones in the lead reached the bottom of the stairs, spilling onto the hall and giving chase as Claude and I shuffled/ran for the doors.

'Cut them off!' shouted the Sandman from his lofty position above us.

Claude swung a backhand haymaker that lifted someone from his feet when he stepped in our path. Whoever it was didn't hit the floor again for about two seconds and when they landed, they didn't move.

Claude's pace was the reason they caught up to me. That and my refusal to leave him behind.

They came, one here and one there, converging from my left and right. I couldn't outrun them, which left me no choice other than to parry their grasping hands. But turning to chop at the throat of one and throw him bodily at another stalled my forward motion. Consequently, the next two, three ... I don't know how many, were on me in the next second.

A hard punch cracked across my jaw and a kick deadened my left thigh. We were almost at the door – it was another yard or so but might as well have been a mile gap across a deep chasm.

I wasn't going to get there.

Bowled over and down onto my back by sheer weight of numbers, it was only because there were so many trying to get to me in an uncoordinated attack that I survived at all. Those still on their feet couldn't kick me now I was down, because there were three bodies on top of me all trying to get enough leverage to deliver a punch.

A huge hand gripped the back of my collar and with a yank that played havoc with my shorts, Claude hauled me from the bottom of the pile with his one good hand.

With a yell of, 'Hold on!' he swung me around like the lady in an ice-skating pair, my feet knocking my attackers down like pins.

It bought us the second of time we needed, so when he set me back down, my whole world still spinning, I threw myself through the gate, reversed direction, and slammed it shut once Claude fell through behind me.

It hit home and locked with a resounding clang when I activated the lock again with the electronic key.

Time to breathe a sigh of relief?

No, because in the half second I paused, a dozen hands came through the bars to loop around my arms, neck, head and chest. They were going to squeeze the life out of me.

Escaped Prisoners

SUNDAY, MAY 14TH 0021HRS

I wanted to call for Claude to help me, but there was a hand clamping my throat so tightly, I couldn't possibly make a noise. My cellmate was bent double from the effort and pain, the blood rushing to his head and the deafening noise of the jeering inmates now trapped inside C Wing enough that he couldn't hear my struggles.

For the second time in the last fifteen minutes, sparkly lights started to dance in front of my eyes.

Finally, Claude looked up.

His shocked face uttered several choice expletives, then he used his giant feet to stamp against the arms where they came through the bars. One by one they all let go until just the hand around my neck remained.

I heard the crack as Claude grabbed a finger and snapped it. A squeal right by my head preceded the air rushing back into my lungs.

I staggered away from the bars of the gate, looking back at the murderous faces glaring through it.

My legs were wobbly, I didn't feel like I had much fight left in me, but we had to go.

I slapped Claude's good arm. 'Come on! We have to get to the warden's office. There's no way to tell which of the prison officers might be on Markham's side. The only one I can trust is the warden.'

Armed with the universal key, we opened the next gate and the next one, but the sound of feet rushing our way made us stall.

The guards were coming. Did they know where we were? Markham told Control I was trying to break out and we were going to show up on the cameras at every intersection. Were they heading for me, or for C Wing to control the riot?

We ducked down a passageway, tucking ourselves out of sight and hoping for the best. They didn't see us, but we both heard their chatter.

The prisoners in C Wing had broken through one of the emergency escape routes – even a prison has to have a way out in case of fire. They were on the roof and in the yard and causing havoc. There wasn't a fire when I triggered the alarm but apparently there were several now.

That was a problem, but it wasn't one I could do anything about. My aim was still to get to the warden.

We gave the guards a few seconds, making sure there were no stragglers before setting off once more. The warden's office is way over on the other side of the prison, close to the main entrance so visiting persons wouldn't have far to go to find him. It meant a half hour journey when I was escorted there previously.

Claude and I covered it in ten.

The prison was in utter disarray. We had to hide from

guards a further four times as they rushed by on their way to somewhere. They were being diverted from other parts of the prison where the inmates were reliably still locked up. There really were fires; we caught a glimpse of bright orange light flickering behind windows when one passageway took us to the inner wall that surrounded the yard in the centre of the prison.

The fire brigade would have to deal with it, but how complex was that when the fire's location was overrun with criminals?

My heartrate had come back down to something close to normal by the time we neared the front of the prison. No one had tried to kill me for several minutes and I was beginning to allow myself to believe we could pull this off.

Yes, technically, we were escaped prisoners, but since we were still inside the prison and would happily give ourselves up to anyone we thought we could trust, I hoped our flight from C Wing wouldn't be held against us.

I peered around the final corner. There were a pair of guards outside the warden's office. They looked like they were there to protect him. Could they be trusted? Or were they part of Markham's gang?

I rationalised that they were probably good guys, or they might already be elsewhere and up to no good.

Just as I was about to step out into the passageway and into plain view, I paused. I'd been about to beg that they hand me over to the warden, but something pinged a warning in my head.

'Markham wanted to take me to the warden's office.'

I said the words out loud and the guards outside the warden's office heard me.

Claude looked down from the rafters, a questioning look on his face.

I nodded to myself. 'He could feel the golem thing coming apart, but he needed to use it again to kill off the final pieces of opposition. The police were already investigating Hyde's death. They were going to figure out the truth in the end, but he had the opportunity to frame you as the golem. He kills you, gets hailed a hero, and takes over the prison drug trade.'

Claude interrupted me, 'Um, Tempest, those two guards are coming.'

They jumped out as he said it, filling the passageway with batons extended.

I looked up at my giant cellmate. 'So hit them for me, Claude. What are you good for?'

I got a surprised look in response, but his good arm flashed out twice in the next second. Launching both prison officers into the wall opposite.

Looking perplexed, he said, 'That's going to add five years to my sentence.'

I argued as I stepped over their legs on my way to the warden's office, 'They are with Markham.'

'How can you be so sure?'

'Because Markham also planned to kill me. He needed me out of the way because he believed I was going to work it out if I hung around long enough. He even said so himself. He was very generous about my detective skills. Markham was bringing me to the warden's office where he planned to kill the warden and then me. He would make it look like I escaped and killed the warden only to then get caught by him. I expect his plan was to murder me. Those two,' I jerked a thumb at the unconscious forms on the carpet behind us, 'were there to keep the warden where Markham wanted him.'

'Good thing we got there first then,' said Claude.

At the door to the warden's office, I grabbed the handle to let myself in.

I was not prepared for what I found inside.

The Only Way to Beat a Golem

SUNDAY, MAY 14TH 0026HRS

The warden was slumped on the carpet in the middle of his office. By his hand, one of the crystal tumblers, the contents spilled on the rug. The brandy decanter was sitting on his desk, a bright red smear of blood on one corner. From an ashtray a foot away from it, smoke from one of his cigars drifted toward the ceiling curling and roiling on the warm air current it created.

I rushed forward, hoping I could still save him and broke one of the most basic rules of house clearance. When you go room to room in a hostile environment, looking for the enemy in close quarters, you always, always check the corners.

The door slammed shut behind me and the next thing I heard was a loud thump followed by the terrible wet sack sound of Claude's unconscious body hitting the rug.

I spun around and backed up to the desk, stepping over the warden's fallen form as I stared at his killers.

We hadn't beaten Markham here at all. He was behind the door with the golem when I came in.

Markham wagged a finger at me. 'Naughty, naughty, Michaels. You just killed the warden. You brought the golem with you and would have escaped if it wasn't for the plucky guard who risked his life to stop you. It's a big spooky mystery, the press and everyone else will believe every word just because it's you.'

Claude wasn't moving; I wasn't getting any help from him. I was on my own and facing two men who were both bigger and stronger than me. They were also used to working as a team.

The only way out of the office was through the door they now blocked with their bodies. I backed up another foot, running options through my head.

The golem spoke for the first time, drawing my focus his way. 'You busted my hand, man. I'm going to make you pay.'

'You can't,' argued Markham. 'It needs to look like I killed him. He and I already look like we have been in a fight because we have. I just need to throttle him now. A sleeper hold that went wrong. That will do it.'

'Arrrrgh, I want to tear his arms off!' raged the golem.

I reached behind me, my hands carefully fumbling for things on the desk.

With a twisted smile that had no place in my current situation, I interrupted their argument.

'You know, I spoke to a friend yesterday. He's an expert on the occult and all things supernatural. He told me there really is only one way to defeat a golem.'

The golem laughed at me. 'Oh yeah? What's that then?'

I showed him the brandy.

'Fire.'

I smashed the top off the decanter on the edge of the desk and spun around before he could move. The dark liquid coated him, dripping from his face, chest, and belly for a heartbeat before the cigar flicked from my hand to ignite it all.

The confident look was gone from his face before the fire even lit. He was a fireball in an instant, and though there wasn't enough brandy to do the job properly, and even though he still had a coating of clay on him, he was going to have severe burns before he could do anything to put out the flames.

Stunned into horrified silence as the golem went up in a squeal of agonising fire, Markham never saw me coming.

I didn't think I could beat him, not in a straight up fight. However, I like to think I can learn and adapt on the hoof. I leapt at his head, wrapping my right arm around his throat, and pulling it in tight with my left.

I had him in the sleeper hold before he knew what I was doing. The question was whether I could keep it on long enough to work.

Markham thrashed, trying to throw me loose.

The golem flailed, a loose arm striking both me and Markham. It sent us backward where Markham crushed me against the wall.

My ribs screamed with pain and my consciousness rebelled, but I held on, never letting my grip falter.

Markham went down to one knee, the fight going from him just as the golem thought to drop and roll.

His flames were almost out but his skin was smoking, and I could see the terrible damage I had done. His chest and stomach caught the worst of it. The clay was gone and, in its place, charred flesh and open bleeding sores ruled.

I had time to look at him and judge whether he was down or not as the fight slowly went out of Markham. I kept the hold on a while longer to be doubly sure, and honestly, I briefly considered not letting go until he was dead.

However, when Claude groaned, and I saw one of his hands move, I released Markham and crawled across to see how badly my cellmate was injured.

I helped him to roll onto his back and then sit up. He had a lump the size of a coffee mug on the side of his skull, but he didn't seem concussed.

Moving to the warden, I heard voices outside, urgent ones that sounded like people arriving.

I got enough time to check the warden's neck and confirm he had a pulse before the door burst open and a face I never wanted to see again sneered down at me.

'Mr Michaels. I might have known.'

Redemption

SUNDAY, MAY 14TH 0132HRS

I groaned and let my head fall back against the wall.

'Quinn. Why did it have to be Quinn?'

As officers swarmed around him, Chief Inspector Quinn directed them to check the warden, the obvious man in the prison officer uniform and the barely conscious and currently whimpering burn victim lying a few feet away.

Perhaps it was that Claude and I looked less in need of medical attention than the others, but I suspected Quinn made sure everyone else was getting dealt with first because he desperately wanted to snub me.

The worst part of that was, if I reacted to his snubbing in any way, he won.

So I sat there, propped against the wall, and took it.

Finally turning his attention my way, Quinn said, 'Make sure you cuff him.'

I didn't bother to resist, holding my hands out so whoever was going to get to me first could do the deed. Cuffs didn't mean a gag though.

'Quinn, you realise we just stopped a jail break, defeated

a murderer, interrupted the drug flow into Maidstone Prison and solved the whole damned case.'

He raised an ironic eyebrow, smiling at me as if I were a great comedian telling jokes.

'Really, Mr Michaels. All that, eh? To me it would appear that you have broken out of your cell, the maximum-security wing, and into the warden's office where I find you in the company of a giant man covered in clay. You are aware I have a detective looking into a murder case where the prime suspect is recorded with such a description, yes? I also find a prison guard unconscious at your feet and a prison in utter turmoil.' He shifted his gaze upward to one of his sergeants. 'Put them somewhere secure.'

'We are both injured,' I pointed out through gritted teeth.

Quinn choked out a laugh. 'Everyone around you seems to be far worse off.'

I met his eyes. 'That's because, with the exception of the warden, they had it coming. Does that sound familiar, Ian?' My voice was a low growl and no one in the room missed my thinly veiled threat.

Dismissively, Quinn said, 'Make sure the paramedics take a look at them when they have dealt with those more severely injured.'

An hour later, Claude and I were both handcuffed to stretchers in a makeshift situation management area in the big yard in the middle of the prison.

No one was telling us anything, but we had at least been treated and made comfortable. They gave us water, and a pair of paramedics checked both of us over. The short version is that we were both going to live. Recovery might take a few weeks, probably more in Claude's case.

We were inside a hastily erected marquee so whatever

was going on outside, we couldn't see. Police were going here and there, coming in and going out, and there were other inmates being brought in for treatment.

When eventually someone came our way, I looked up to see it was Detective Sergeant Atwell. He had a tired, weather-beaten look about him, but he offered me a wave and half smile as he crossed the marquee.

His first words were, 'The warden came around,' and his second sentence was, 'Quinn was not happy to hear that you're the good guy in all this.'

It was news that made me smile.

Claude and I listened intently as the ageing detective explained what he knew. It transpired that according to the warden, I was an unwitting part of a sting operation to flush out crooked guards he and Superintendent Yardley were convinced were working with Henry Featherstone. They had been trying to infiltrate those involved in the movement of drugs in the prison for more than a year but had no idea Markham might be involved.

The golem thing threw them a curveball, forcing them to step up their plans and that was where I came in. Suddenly they had a paranormal detective inside the prison and a way to shake things up. The warden had apparently expressed a deep regret that I had come so close to getting killed. He had no idea so many of his guards were dirty.

Markham had chosen to stick with his story about trying to stop me after he discovered I was handling the golem, but the presence of two golems left him struggling to explain it all and there were huge holes in his tale. Then his brother – that's who the real golem was - high on morphine, told the police absolutely everything on his way to the hospital.

Markham was in custody.

They found Superintendent Yardley unconscious in a

cell. Mike Atwell's guess was they planned to frame me for his murder too. It was all very neat. Claude was the golem, I was the deranged paranormal expert who knew all about the legend and how to manipulate it, and Markham was the hero prison officer who stopped us both. Originally, he planned to take out his opponents and anyone who stood in the way of him taking over the drug trade. The golem would then have vanished. My poking around changed that.

Needing to kill me, he chose to remove the warden and Yardley and give the police a golem to arrest for Hyde's murder.

Mike removed my cuffs, but I wasn't going home. I still had over six weeks to serve. I shook hands with Claude and wished him inner peace. I didn't know what was in his past, but if he really had killed his wife, he seemed truly sorry and content somehow that he was where he deserved to be.

I was going back to minimum security.

I hoped there was French toast for breakfast.

Afterword

Those readers who follow me and read these notes, will know that I write by the seat of my pants. The industry even has a term for writers like me: I'm a pantser. The opposite end of the spectrum is a plotter. At the extreme end, some writers who plot have meticulous notes listing what is going to happen in each chapter, how long each chapter should be et cetera. I usually have a scribbled page of A4 with a few notes because I've thought of something really cool that should happen.

This novella – according to the industry, anything over twenty-five thousand words is a novella – was supposed to be a short story. It was going to be five thousand words or maybe a little more. That's what I get for being a pantser, but I think it's more exciting to write like this.

As Tempest was my first creation, and he is largely based on me, I feel very much at home writing his adventures. I think of myself as a cozy mystery author, but it is always refreshing to return to the Blue Moon cast.

Maidstone prison really does sit right in the middle of

the city centre. It is this giant high-walled structure with a huge stone wall at one end of the central business district. I have always imagined it must be an additional form of punishment for the inmates inside to hear the people in the bars across the street and be able to smell the food cooking in the venues mere yards away. I was accurate with the age of the prison, but all the other details were created in my head. They do not have minimum and maximum-security wings in the same prison; I'm not sure they do that anywhere, but it was necessary here for the story to work.

The superman punch, just in case that term is not one you are familiar with, is also a real thing. It's not easy to get right, and I haven't attempted one since I was in my thirties.

You may have noticed that I jumped the timeline forward by six months. Until this book, the stories have followed on almost immediately after the previous one finished. The previous sixteen books covered a period of less than four months unless one includes *Under a Blue Moon* which I wrote as a prequel and set six months earlier.

There is a reason for this leap, and there will be another jump now to the next book which will occur once Tempest is released from prison in late summer. Primarily, this is because I wish to align the timelines.

I wrote two crossover books with Tempest Michaels working alongside Patricia Fisher. They operate in the same fictional world, but the events with Patricia were set a year on from the Blue Moon books I have already written. I want to catch up with myself.

Why? I imagine you asking. Because I have an idea for a storyline that will combine four different series and bring them all together to solve one problem. Honestly, I'm not sure I am bright enough to pull it off, but if I can, Patricia,

Albert and Rex, Felicity, and Tempest will all collide in one book.

There will be other crossovers, but the other three series all occur at the same point in time. Only Tempest and his crew were out of synch which is what happens when you write by the seat of your pants and have no idea what you might dream up next.

Take care.

Steve Higgs

Next in the Blue Moon Investigations Series

vinci-books.com/sparks-darkness

Fire.

Every creature fears it.

Except one.

When a call late one evening leads Jane to Buckingham Palace, she isn't concerned that the dragon they want her to investigate is real.

Until she gets there, that is.

Turn the page for a free preview…

Sparks in the Darkness: Chapter One

A NEW ENTRY ON THE CHART

Thursday, October 12th 1812hrs

I had to fight to stop the yawn that was threatening to split my head in two. The phone was ringing, insistently demanding I answer it. Yet even though I could pick it up and thumb the green button to connect the call, there was no way I could speak until I wrestled my fatigue under control.

Worried the caller might ring off if I let it go to voicemail, I touched the green button anyway.

A second ticked by as the caller waited for someone to speak. My jaw was still wide open, and I considered using both hands to force it shut.

'Hello?' a woman's voice rang through loud and clear. As my yawn finally subsided, I noted the clear, precise nature of the woman's accent. More correctly, I should say that her voice was without an accent, which is to say I heard no regional markers to place her from the west or the north or from a particular county. Rather, she just sounded posh to my ears, her upbringing one that might have involved private schools and Bentleys.

I was filling in a lot of blanks with silly imagined scenarios as I fought to get my teeth aligned so I could finally speak.

'Hello?' the woman repeated herself. 'Is there anyone there?'

'Yes, sorry,' I blurted. 'This is Jane Butterworth. Good evening and welcome to the Blue Moon Paranormal Detective Agency. How may I help you?'

'Is this call being recorded?' she asked, the question direct and demanding.

'Um, no,' I lied, turning off the recorder I habitually use.

I heard the woman exhale. 'Very well. My name is Detective Inspector Munroe. I am calling you from Buckingham Palace.'

'Buckingham Palace?' I questioned. 'Where the Queen lives?'

'The Queen is not in residence and rarely stays in Buckingham Palace,' the detective replied matter-of-factly. 'Neither is her majesty a factor in the matter at hand. I require …' the woman fell silent, giving me the impression she was wrestling with how to frame what she wanted to say.

This is not all that unusual in my line of work. As you probably gathered from the title of the firm, we specialise in paranormal investigations. Blue Moon was started by my boss, though I should probably refer to him as my colleague now. I am one of three detectives working at the agency. We have an office on Rochester High Street just a stone's throw from the cathedral. I came to the firm as an assistant to do the general administration tasks. However, after dabbling in a case because there was no one else to tackle it, I was swiftly promoted, and now get my own cases.

Before the police officer could speak again, I tried to finish her sentence. 'You have unexplainable events at the palace, and you need to hire a specialist who can be quiet and discreet.'

I got to hear DI Munroe sigh with relief. 'Yes, exactly that. Discretion is paramount in this matter.'

'Can you tell me what has occurred?' I begged.

Honestly, I expected her to regale me with a story of a ghost or a mysterious noise in the walls. Given that everything we deal with fell somewhere on the weirdometer, you can imagine how rarely I hear something that surprises me.

However, when she began explaining her problem, I was forced to interrupt. 'I'm sorry, you have a what?' I couldn't help but ask.

'A dragon,' DI Munroe repeated her previous words. 'At least, it flies and breathes fire, and I don't know what else to call it.'

Right. A dragon.

Swapping my phone from right hand to left, I crossed the office to the wall where we have a chart. Tempest – my boss – created it one night as a bit of fun. On the chart are our three names and beneath each are rows which list various creatures. There are ghosts, vampires, werewolves, pixies ... you name it, and you can bet someone has called us to investigate one at some point. I was behind on werewolves, failing to score even one case yet, and Amanda was the only one who could claim to have been called to solve an alien-based mystery.

However, I took the handy pen set next to the chart and added a new row, writing the word dragon and putting a big tick under my name.

'Am I correct to assume you would like me to come now?' I checked.

DI Munroe replied instantly. 'Of course, Miss Butterworth ... Is it Miss?' she asked, checking my marital status.

I almost told her that I'm actually a mister, but revealing my true gender when I am dressed and acting as Jane would do me no favours, so I brushed the question to one side.

'Jane will do. I shall leave immediately. How do I gain access to the palace? Is there a way in with my car?'

I listened intently, switching on the recorder again to catch her instructions as she relayed where I needed to go and how to avoid getting shot by the soldiers guarding the palace gates.

With the call ended and my car keys in my hand, I checked the office front door was secure and went out the back. I was going to Buckingham Palace.

Sparks in the Darkness: Chapter Two

ROYAL TARGETS

Thursday, October 12th 1927hrs

DI Munroe called me before I arrived, anxious to check on my progress. Consequently, she met me at the gate when I revealed I was only a few minutes from arriving. It made getting through the gate easy at least.

'Nice car,' she commented, sliding into the passenger seat of my Aston Martin to guide me through the palace grounds.

'It was a gift,' I admitted. I could never afford to buy such an extravagant car, not least because it was one of the stunt models made for the James Bond Movie, *The Living Daylights*, and still had all the secret buttons and devices on it. Not that the machine guns fired real bullets, they were just props, but it was fun to know I could press a button and have them pop up from the bonnet.

Munroe showed me where to park and started to fill me in on her problem.

'It started more than a week ago.'

'A week?' I questioned, amazed they had let it go on for so long.

'I didn't know what it was at the time.' She took a breath and plunged on. 'We found a body. It was one of the soldiers. A young private in the Grenadier Guards by the name of Karl Matthewson. He completed his two-hour watch and was relieved, but failed to return to the guard house. When the soldiers went looking for him, they found his charred remains. He was still clutching his rifle but hadn't managed to get a shot off.'

I stayed silent, noting everything she said in my head because she refused to let me record her or even write anything down.

'I was called at that point. I have quarters in the grounds of the palace,' she explained. 'It was ... is my job to investigate, but I will unhappily admit I have no idea what happened to the man. He wasn't near a source of fire, and I am not willing to believe in self-combustion.'

A memory surfaced, jolting me to focus on it. Months ago, we had a case where a man had self-combusted. We investigated on behalf of the family and there were other reports at the time that led us to believe there was a person messing around with fire.

Not your standard arsonist or pyromaniac though, this was something different. This was ... magical almost, like there was a person who could create, control, and manipulate fire. The trail went cold, and the case remained unsolved.

So far.

I dragged my thoughts back to the present because DI Munroe was still talking.

'After three days of expert opinion, forensic examination, and painstaking investigation, I had achieved nothing, but then one of the soldiers spotted something inside the palace grounds.'

I kept quiet, desperate to ask questions, but unwilling to interrupt her.

'There was a figure on the roof. Lance Corporal McKinnon's report states that it was a black figure with glowing orange eyes. He also said it had wings, though when I pressed him, he admitted he couldn't be sure about the last part. His words were corroborated by Guardsman Bartlet who was with him. They challenged it and raised the alarm before giving chase. They have a quick reaction force here at all times – it's a standard military thing apparently. The QRF as they call themselves, deployed within seconds, swarming the palace in a bid to cut off the intruder.'

'They didn't catch it,' I supplied, finding myself drawn into her tale.

'No,' she agreed. 'But with pressure from the palace to resolve this issue, and the press sniffing around because the family of the dead soldier are demanding answers, I gave up trying to do this myself and called you.' We were out of my car and walking across the moonlit palace grounds on our way to get inside when DI Munroe abruptly stopped moving.

I turned to face her to find her staring right at me. I guess she felt this part of her story required eye to eye contact so I would know how serious she was.

'The soldiers caught up to the … thing on the roof. It was less than fifty yards from the Queen's bedroom. They opened fire when it disobeyed their challenge and vanished into the shadows. When they saw it again a few seconds later, they resumed firing.'

'They shot it?' I questioned, wondering what I was doing here if the thing they wanted my advice on was already dead.

'The bullets had no effect.' DI Munroe looked scared as she retold her story. 'According to the after-action report – that's what the soldiers call it – the ... dragon smashed through a window and set the curtains on fire, torching the room it went into so the soldiers could not follow.'

I could feel my own pulse rising, the startling nature of this case causing a creeping sense of self-doubt and worry to spread like chilled water through my veins.

'The soldiers were unsure what to do at that point. They never go inside the palace, and I think they hesitated before smashing windows in an adjacent room so they could follow. When they did, they discovered another body, this time one of the palace stewards. He was in the hallway outside the room the dragon broke in through. Wrong place at the wrong time. The QRF fanned out, going room to room as they attempted to find the beast. It was a mercy it didn't get to the members of the royal family currently in residence or ... well, you can imagine the headlines if someone broke in and killed the heir to the throne.'

I could indeed, but had a question. 'Who is in residence?'

'Since that second attack, almost no one. There were senior figures here, including the heir to the throne who was in London to host a big event for one of his charities. He was removed to a safer location within hours of the first incursion. Most of the others left shortly thereafter. Only one is still here, Lord Edward Chamberlain, second son of Duke Westborough. The duke is twelfth in line to the throne after Prince Charles, his sons, and Prince Charles' grandchildren. That makes Lord Chamberlain technically fourteenth in line to the throne, but he is far enough down the peerage that he doesn't get any special protection.'

'He is still here despite the attack?' I questioned.

DI Munroe nodded. 'Yes, he's quite cavalier about it and claims to see no danger. I know the palace wanted him to go but he declined. I am left with the belief he likes being the only royal in residence. Anyway,' she sucked in a deep breath, 'we've been digressing from the topic at hand, and we are yet to get to the best part.'

I cranked an eyebrow, wondering what was going to top the fire breathing dragon.

DI Munroe didn't make me wait. 'I am under orders to sew this up without the press ever knowing about it, but I'm not sure if that is going to be possible.'

'Why not?' I asked, my brow wrinkling with confusion.

DI Munroe pursed her lips and sighed deeply. 'Because of what happened next. The soldiers worked across the palace covering the top two levels in a systematic sweep. They did a great job at enormous personal risk and cornered the *dragon*,' it was clear from the way she said the word that she could scarcely believe it herself, 'as it made its way back to the roof. Then,' she sucked in a deep breath, 'it flew.'

'It flew?'

She nodded. 'That is what more than two dozen soldiers claim. It opened its wings and took off into the night sky. Two of the guardsmen opened fire, their rounds having no effect again. Mercifully, their commander ordered them to cease fire. He was rightly concerned the bullets would come to land in the grounds outside the palace – there are houses nearby and people going past at all times of the day and night.'

I did my best to summarise.

'We have a creature who is bulletproof, able to spew fire, and it can fly. Anything else?'

'Orange eyes,' DI Munroe reminded me. 'They estimated its height at about six feet and described it as able to defy gravity. I don't know what it is, but after the second attack ... well, let's just say I am under pressure to prevent a third incident from occurring.'

I watched the detective's face. There was something she wasn't telling me. Something about her personal motivations behind calling a paranormal investigator for help.

'Do you believe it is a dragon?' I sought to clarify.

The detective shrugged. 'I don't know what to think. I can get my head around the bulletproof and the flame thing, but the flying is hard to explain. Whatever my personal thoughts on the matter, my bosses will not entertain the idea that there is a supernatural creature plaguing the palace and if I suggest otherwise, I'll need a new job.'

There it was. That sense of something hidden.

'Why would they take your job away?' I challenged her. She was keeping something secret, and I hated not knowing all the parameters when I go into an investigation. It is like trying to read while looking through gauze.

DI Munroe sucked in a breath as she frowned and was about to give me a dismissive answer when I raised a knowing eyebrow and folded my arms. Her words caught in her throat, and I got to see her shoulders slump.

'It is not germane to the case,' she stated. 'But ... look, this is a punishment post for me. You don't need to know the details, but if I don't sew this up quickly, or if I give my boss any just cause to question my ability, he will fire me.'

Enough said. There was something in her past that

placed her on a bad footing. She came across as a little desperate and as she started walking again, I fell into step by her side.

It was time to see what clues she might have uncovered.

**Grab your copy...
vinci-books.com/sparks-darkness**

About the Author

When Steve Higgs wrote his debut novel, *Paranormal Nonsense*, he was a captain in the British Army. He would like to pretend that he had one of those careers that must be blacked out and generally denied by the government, and that he has to change his name and move constantly because he is still on the watch list in several countries. In truth, though, he started out as a mechanic - not like Jason Statham in the film by that name, sneaking around as a hitman, but more like one of those sleazy guys who charges a fortune and keeps your car for a week even though the only thing you went in for was a squeaky door hinge.

At school, he was largely disinterested in all subjects except creative writing, for which he won his first prize at the age of ten. However, calling it the first prize he won suggests that there were other prizes, which is not the case. Awards may yet come, but in the meantime, he enjoys writing mystery and thriller novels and claims to have more than a hundred books forming a restless queue in his mind because they are desperate to be written.

Now retired from the military, he lives in southeast England with a duo of lazy sausage dogs. Surrounded by rolling hills, brooding castles, and vineyards, he doubts he'll ever leave, the beer is just too good.

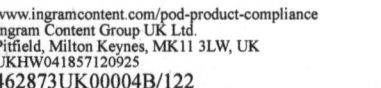

www.ingramcontent.com/pod-product-compliance
Ingram Content Group UK Ltd.
Pitfield, Milton Keynes, MK11 3LW, UK
UKHW041857120925
462873UK00004B/122